MURPHY'S WRATH

MURPHY'S LAW BOOK TWO

MICHELLE ST. JAMES

BLACKTHORN PRESS

MURPHY'S WRATH

Murphy's Law Book Two

Michelle St. James

This is a work of fiction. Any resemblance to actual persons, living or dead, events, or locales is entirely coincidental.

Copyright 2019 by Michelle St. James aka Michelle Zink

All rights reserved.

Cover design by Isabel Robalo

1

Ronan Murphy watched his brother's face through the shadows inside the car. "See anything?"

Nick lowered the binoculars. "Tell you what: I'll let you know if I see anything so you can stop asking me every ten minutes. Or better yet," he held out the binoculars to Ronan, "you can look for yourself."

Ronan took the binoculars, even though he'd handed them to Nick two hours earlier precisely because he'd gotten sick of peering through them and seeing nothing unusual.

They'd been casing Connor Moran's office for almost a week. Like all of Ronan's recent targets in his effort to find Elise Berenger, Congressman Moran had appeared on the list of the Whitmore Club's membership, but he also occupied a place on their board. Ronan had no idea how the shadowy group called Manifest was linked to the Whitmore Club, but it undoubtedly was, and as far as Ronan was concerned a board member was more likely to be involved.

That's what he'd told himself when they'd started staking out the Whitmore's board members, anyway. So far it had amounted to almost nothing.

He'd never been as frustrated with a case as he'd been in the three months since he and Julia came home from Dubai without Julia's sister, Elise.

He'd been sure Elise was at Gold, the club in Dubai linked to Manifest. He was still sure she'd been there, although it wasn't something he said aloud to Julia. Everything about the place had screamed wealth and secrecy, and he'd been haunted by the well-heeled couple who'd been sitting outside the private offices on the top floor of the club, a steel briefcase on the table in front of them.

Had the couple been there to buy a girl? To buy Elise?

Rumors were rampant online about the secret society called Manifest: that they engaged in trafficking, that they were backed by a consortium of rich, powerful men, that they influenced politics with money and blackmail and a host of other unsavory methods.

It was something he didn't let himself consider too often. The curtain of rage that spilled over his vision made it hard to think straight, rivaled only by the helplessness he felt when he caught Julia's expression in an unguarded moment. It was fear and pain so raw he sometimes had to stifle a primal scream, her pain fostering his fury until his need to make Manifest pay eclipsed the reason he'd spent a lifetime cultivating.

He tried not to think about the way she'd fought as he'd carried her out of Gold, gunfire erupting around them as she yelled for Elise and called Ronan names. He'd hated it, but every instinct in his body had told him his only job was to get Julia out of there alive.

The owners of Gold had proven difficult to crack, even for the world-class hackers kept on retainer by Murphy Intelligence and Security. Whoever Gold's owners were, they were tied to Manifest, hidden behind a network of shell companies and fake identities that MIS was still trying to unravel.

They'd diversified their strategy six weeks earlier by refocusing on the members of the Whitmore Club. They proved easier to target — technically the place was an aboveboard private club for Boston's wealthy movers and shakers — but the ease of getting the information was offset by the sheer number of leads it opened up. Every member had multiple businesses and places of residences, associations that fanned out into overlapping patterns that took up a whole wall in the MIS conference room.

Their hackers were still working the Dubai angle, but in the meantime, Ronan had been doing recon on every long-standing member of the Whitmore Club, staking out their houses and places of businesses, running background on every known associate.

He tried to ignore the feeling that he was spinning his wheels, that the activity was doing little more than keeping him moving, allowing him to convince Julia they were making progress when any fool could see they were at a standstill.

And Julia Berenger was no fool.

"We can't do this forever."

Ronan turned toward his brother's voice. Nick was staring out the windshield, his eyes focused on the brick facade of the Congressman's downtown office.

"We fucking can and will," Ronan said.

Nick looked at Ronan, his green eyes flashing in

the dim light of the street lamps around the car. "No, we can't. The Berenger job never fell within our core service offerings, and we've been at it for more than three months. We have other clients waiting."

"Core service offerings? You sound like such an asshole."

Nick shrugged. "Somebody's got to do it. It used to be you."

Ronan heard the meaning flowing under Nick's words like a current: that Ronan had gotten soft, that he wasn't being professional, that his feelings for Julia were clouding his judgement. "Careful, Nick."

He hoped Nick heard the warning in his words, hoped it was a warning Nick heeded. It had been a long time since they'd fought it out, but Ronan wasn't too old to kick Nick's ass.

Nick moved his shoulders like he was loosening the kinks. "I'm not saying anything you don't know — and for the record, I'm not saying anything Dec doesn't agree with."

Ronan's laugh was short. "Criticism from Declan doesn't exactly hit me where it hurts."

Knowing each other too well was just one of many perils of working with one's siblings. As a former cop with Boston PD — following in their father's footsteps — Nick was perfectly capable of stepping in when things got hot in the field, but Ronan did most of the dirty work, along with the high-level strategizing, both areas of expertise a product of his time as a Navy SEAL.

Nick had seemed to surprise even himself when he'd realized he was good at managing the business side of things. He had a knack for dealing with the financials, crossing every T and dotting every I with the IRS while stashing money in lucrative investments and offshore accounts that had made them all millionaires many times over.

Sometimes Ronan thought it was a shame. Nick had been a great beat cop and an even better detective, thriving on the excitement and danger of criminal work in a city as complex as Boston. More than once Ronan had wondered if it was because of Erin, their sister who'd overdosed when he and Nick had been in their early twenties. Maybe seeing all that crime up close and personal had been too much. Ronan wouldn't know: as brothers went, he and Nick were close, but none of the Murphy brothers were eager to pick the scab off the wound of their dead sister, and that included Declan, an aimless douchebag either by birth or through the circumstances of their mother's death from cancer followed by Erin's overdose.

Dec was an equal partner in the business, but while he showed an annoying level of competence at pretty much anything when pressed into duty, he couldn't be pressed into duty often between the bevy of women who frequented his bed at their shared residence.

"Dec's not stupid," Nick said, pulling Ronan from his thoughts.

"I didn't say he was," Ronan said. "But we both know he's not in a position to criticize."

Nick met his eyes. "We're all in a position to criticize, Ro. That's what it means to have partners. And brothers."

Ronan looked away, not wanting to admit Nick was right. What would Ronan do if the roles were reversed? If Nick deployed the company on what was, for all intents and purposes, a wild goose chase, tying up their resources in a pro bono client while paying clients waited in the wings?

He didn't have to think long about the question. Ronan would shut it down. He'd tell Nick exactly what Nick was telling him, albeit a lot less diplomatically. Their business, borne out of their grief and rage over Erin's death, was about more than money, but they couldn't take pro bono jobs without paid clients.

"Clay and his guys are getting close to something on Gold," Ronan said. Clay was the unofficial leader of their freelance digital team and the hacker who'd gotten them deeper into the Manifest website when Ronan had first met Julia.

"That's what you said last month."

"It was true last month." Ronan looked at Nick. "This isn't some hit job. We knew it would be more complicated going in."

The Berenger job had always been outside of MIS's true purview. For lack of a more eloquent word, they were vigilantes, men who stepped in to take out the trash when the system had failed, as it had when it set loose the drug dealer who'd gotten Erin hooked on heroin when she was still in high school.

They weren't private investigators. Clients came to them when they already knew who to punish.

But Ronan had been moved by John Taylor's predicament even before he'd crashed into Julia in an alley, both of them surveilling Seth Campbell, the tech giant who'd been dating Elise before her disappearance. At the time Ronan hadn't known Julia was his new client's granddaughter any more than Julia had known her grandfather, John Taylor, had hired MIS to find Elise and punish her kidnappers.

Usually MIS was called in when it was too late to save anyone. By the time their clients walked through the doors of their office, the damage had been done.

All that was left was retribution.

John Taylor was everything Ronan admired: a quiet but commanding man of few words, a former Army drill sergeant, a man who took seriously his duty to protect the people he loved, even if it meant subverting the law.

In Taylor's plea, Ronan had seen an opportunity to actually save someone, to save Elise Berenger before punishing the men who'd taken her.

Had he been compromised by his history, by the loss of Erin all those years ago, by his inability to save her? Fuck yes. That's all MIS was: a series of attempts at rewriting a history that could never be rewritten.

It hadn't stopped them from taking jobs before.

"I'm concerned about the personal angle," Nick said. "And before you get your panties in a twist, you know you'd say the same thing to me if the roles were reversed."

Ronan bit back his anger, forced himself to breathe. The personal angle. It was too antiseptic a word for the feelings he had for Julia Berenger.

She flashed behind his eyelids: her tawny hair spread like silk across his bare chest, body supple and soft in his arms, brown eyes lit with amber fire and pain she didn't want him to see.

"We made a commitment to John Taylor." Ronan wouldn't pretend Julia had nothing to do with his desire to find Elise, but their contract — illegal and unspoken as it was — wasn't nothing. In their business, a business not found on Yelp and not reviewed on social media, trust was everything. If they started backing out of every job when it got tough, their paying clients wouldn't be so eager to pay, and that would mean no more pro bono work either, and no more MIS, something that was more than just business for the Murphy brothers.

Nick sighed. "I know. I'm just saying. There has to be an end point. We don't have to figure out what it is tonight, but you should start thinking about it."

An end point: a polite way of saying the point at which they gave up on Elise Berenger, the point at which Ronan would have to tell Julia her sister was lost forever, just like Erin.

Over his dead fucking body.

2

Julia turned off the engine and looked at the cottage in the middle of the clearing bordered by trees. It was August and at least ten degrees cooler here than in the city, but she couldn't seem to make herself move.

The living room light was on in her gramps' house, the glow warm and welcoming, and yet she could only sit, the cold air seeping from the car's interior, the engine ticking as it cooled. It had been like that in the months since she'd gotten back from Dubai, her usual anticipation at seeing her grandfather dampened by the fact that week after week, there was no news about Elise.

Her frustration was only inflamed by her gramps' calmness. It wasn't that he wasn't worried about Elise — he still called hospitals every two days to see if anyone matching Elise's description had been brought in without ID.

But where Julia's panic seemed to rise with each passing day, an invisible clock ticking down the time that had passed since Elise's disappearance (four months, five days, twenty hours) while her runaway mind calculated the decreasing probability that she was still alive, her gramps was unflappable in his belief that Ronan and his brothers would bring Elise home safe and sound.

It should have brought Julia comfort. Her gramps was no fool. If he believed Elise was coming home alive, why couldn't she put her faith in the same belief? Or why couldn't she pretend, at least, during their weekly dinners?

It was easier at the Murphy house. There she didn't dare express even the slightest worry that Elise wasn't alive. She needed MIS to stay invested in Elise's case, and while she knew Ronan wouldn't stop looking, she was less sure about Nick and Declan. As much as she'd come to care about the two younger Murphy brothers — she'd never met the youngest, Finn, who apparently hadn't been home in years — she didn't know them well enough to assume they wouldn't throw in the towel on a case that was going nowhere, for which they weren't being paid a dime.

In their company, she was careful to refer to Elise in the present tense, to speak about her sister as if there was no doubt she was alive and waiting to be rescued.

But her gramps' house had been the one place she could tell the truth when she was scared without worrying it would be used against her later, a favorite tactic of her mother, who'd always been more invested in her latest boyfriend than in Julia and Elise.

Their gramps had taken care of them when their mother couldn't, had protected them from life's uglier realities while never lying to them.

Now Julia couldn't help wondering if he really believed Elise was alive or if, for the first time ever, he was lying to Julia — and maybe even to himself.

The porch light came on and the front door opened, her gramps silhouetted in the doorway. From a distance, he might have been thirty, tall and proud in his Army uniform like in the photographs she'd seen of him when he was younger.

He'd known she was out front of course, had obviously just been giving her time to collect her thoughts before he decided enough was enough.

She stepped out of the car and breathed in the air laced with pine and cooling earth as she made her way up the porch steps. "Hey, gramps."

He wore his uniform of pressed slacks, button-down shirt, and the cardigan she rarely saw him without. His brown eyes shone with affection as he leaned in to kiss her cheek.

"I thought we'd eat on the deck."

"Sounds good," she said, stepping into the house.

"I have lemonade and iced tea," he said. "Unless you'd prefer something stronger."

She laughed. "I'll take lemonade."

Her grandfather disapproved of ready-made food and beverages, lemonade included. His lemonade was fresh-squeezed and mixed with simple syrup that dissolved seamlessly into the liquid.

He went to the cupboard and pulled out two glasses, put an ice cube in each, and poured lemonade from a glass pitcher on the counter.

He slid one of the glasses toward her and raised his own. "To summer, steaks, and fresh lemonade."

She touched her glass to his. "I'll drink to all those things."

"Let me get the salad and we'll head outside."

He set down his glass and removed a bowl from

the fridge. Julia leaned in to get a look and saw that it was her favorite pasta salad, chock full of mozzarella and asparagus and olives in a tangy dressing of blended capers, sun-dried tomatoes, balsamic vinegar, and olive oil.

"Yum, my favorite." This was safe ground. Food, lemonade, summer. It was a lie of sorts. A lie that everything was okay, that they were like everyone else enjoying the last weeks of the season.

Sometimes you needed a lie to survive the truth.

He started for the side door with the pasta salad bowl cradled in his arm. "Bring my glass, will you?"

Was it her imagination that he moved slower than she remembered? That he held onto the bowl a little too tightly, as if he might drop it?

She shook her head against the notion. Her gramps might be seventy-eight years old, but he was as strong as he'd been when he was a drill sergeant, still capable of swearing a blue streak and kicking her ass — figuratively anyway — when she needed it.

She picked up his glass and carried it with her through the French doors leading to the deck off the kitchen.

It was cooler outside, though still pleasant, and

she set the lemonade on the table and watched as her gramps opened the grill.

"Need help?" she asked.

"The day I need help cooking a steak is the day pigs fly, missy."

She smiled. "Just offering."

"Sit down and enjoy the lemonade," he said. The steaks sizzled as he placed them on the hot grill. "There's a blanket on the chair if you get cold."

"You think of everything," she said, settling into one of the teak chairs, her back against the old blanket.

"Anything for my girls."

"Your girl, you mean." The words slipped from her mouth.

He closed the grill, walked over to the table, and took the seat next to her. He placed his hand over hers. "My girls," he repeated. "I'm doing all I can for Elise, and so are you."

"Am I? It doesn't feel that way."

He searched her eyes. "What could you be doing that you aren't doing?"

She searched her mind. How could she tell her grandfather that it felt wrong to be holed up at the Murphy house, surrounded by funny, strong men who made her laugh, who cooked for her and made her feel safe even as her sister was missing and possibly dead?

She gave up with a sigh. "I don't know. It just feels like we should be doing more."

She heard the unspoken accusation in her voice, knew he heard it too when he spoke again.

"You think I'm not doing enough." His hand was still warm on hers.

"You don't seem worried anymore," she said. "It's like you've given up on her."

There. She'd said it, voiced her worst fear, the suspicion that had lurked behind every one of their dinners since she'd returned from Dubai.

"I call the hospitals every other day. I comb the papers for mentions of Jane Does. I offered up my savings to the Murphy's."

Shame heated Julia's face as he stood and walked to the grill. She waited as he flipped the steaks and returned to the table.

"My generation was different than yours," he said. "We didn't talk about things so much, we didn't... examine everything. Some would say we were cold, even repressed. We thought we were strong." He shook his head. "I don't know the right answer, Julia. Would showing my worry help Elise? Would it help you?"

"It won't help Elise," she admitted. "I know that."

"And you?" he asked. "Would it help you?"

"Not really. I guess I just want to know I'm not alone. That I'm not the only one staring at the ceiling at night, wondering if she's okay, if she's hurt or cold or hungry, if she's wondering why we haven't come for her."

"You're not the only one. I'm trying to be strong for her. For you. That's all."

"I'm sorry," she said.

He patted her hand and stood. "Don't be. I may not be a big talker, but I'm always here to listen."

He pulled the steaks off the grill and her stomach rumbled at the smell of cooked meat. She realized she hadn't eaten since breakfast, something that happened more than she wanted to admit when Ronan was out of the house.

Her gramps returned to the table and set a giant steak in front of her. "Bon appetite."

"It looks amazing. Thank you."

She dished herself some pasta salad and dug in. They ate in silence for a few minutes before her gramps spoke again.

"I spoke to your mother yesterday."

Her appetite soured in her stomach. She set down her fork. "Oh?"

Her gramps nodded as he chewed a bite of his steak. "You should pay her a visit. She's worried about Elise, and she'd like to see you."

Julia reached for her lemonade. "I'm not sure I believe either of those things."

"Your mother has her own way," her gramps said. "You know that."

"Boy, do I." Julia couldn't keep the sarcasm from her voice.

"Don't be unkind," he scolded.

It was an old argument. Her gramps wasn't exactly approving of the path Julia's mother had taken, her pattern of dropping everything for the wrong man again and again, of neglecting Julia and Elise while she doted on one loser after another, but Lisa Taylor-Berenger-Burns-Maher was still his daughter.

"I haven't heard from her once since Elise went missing," Julia said. "The last time I talked to her was two days after Elise disappeared."

"You can reach out too."

Julia leaned back in her chair and crossed her arms over her chest. She knew she was acting like a child but couldn't seem to help herself. "Why does it always have to be me?"

"Because you can't change people," he said. "And

trying only frustrates all concerned. Your mother loves you, she just doesn't know how to show it the way you want her too, the way I wish she would. And apparently Ray's out of the picture."

"Now I get it," Julia said. "She's alone again, so it's back to her perpetual Plan B."

After the Plan A of her newest man inevitably failed, Julia and Elise were always their mother's backup plan — for affection, for purpose, for validation.

Her grandfather was silent as he took a bite of his pasta salad, his gaze pulled outward to the trees surrounding the house, their shadows long and deep as the sun sank closer to the horizon.

"It might make you feel better too, you know," he finally said.

"I doubt that. And it's a waste of time anyway. Ray might be gone, but it's only a matter of time before Ray 2.0 steps into the picture. It's not worth rushing the gap. She'll be back to Plan A in no time."

"Forgive me dear, but at what point do you intend to let go of these old hurts?" She looked at him, wounded as always by his insistence on trying to bridge the gap between her and Elise and their mother. Why did it feel like disloyalty? "I have news for you: none of us are perfect. Not even you, although personally, I can't seem to find your fault."

His words softened the crust that had been building around her heart. "Don't be ridiculous. I know I'm not perfect. I just don't see why it's so bad to protect yourself from someone who's hurt you over and over again. Isn't that just self-preservation? Isn't it the smart thing to do?"

Her gramps sighed. "I'm hardly the arbiter on smart, but I will say there's a fine line between self-preservation and avoidance."

She took a bite of her steak as she turned over his words. She'd been telling herself for years that avoiding her mother was the intelligent thing to do. In modern vernacular, her mother was toxic, their relationship damaging to Julia's psyche, her peace of mind.

Had she been lying to herself? Was she just avoiding the painful work of forgiveness, of moving forward?

She wished Elise was there. They would buy wine and hash out their feelings on the sofa in the tiny apartment Julia couldn't bear to live in anymore. Elise, with her breezy tendency to blow off anything that didn't make her feel good, might be more forgiving, but she would understand Julia's perpetual angst over the issue.

There were a million things she wanted to talk to Elise about: Ronan and the way he made her feel, her easy slip into the Murphy household, her affection for serious Nick and devil-may-care Declan, her worry that everything had happened too fast between her and Ronan to be sustainable, that they'd come together under circumstances that had heightened feelings that would otherwise have fizzled.

Despite their differences, Elise had been Julia's confidant. Julia had a few acquaintances from her jobs over the years, and there was Emily Goldberg, a friend from college that she saw a couple times a year when the stars aligned, but without Elise, Julia had no one to talk to about the details of her life that were too intimate to share with her gramps.

She thought about Ronan. He would listen. He would hear her out without judgement.

But she wasn't ready to give him all the sordid details of her fucked up childhood. Not when he looked at her like she was the sun and the moon, like she was perfect and pure. Not when their relationship seemed built on the finest of sand, on the peril they'd faced in Dubai, on their shared mission to find Elise and bring her home.

It was working right now. It was more than working: it was perfect. She didn't want to rock the boat, and she was aware of holding back, of keeping a piece of herself apart from Ronan even as she verbalized her love for him.

It was one thing to say it. It was something else to have faith in it.

She tried not to think about what would happen after they found Elise. Would they settle into a normal life? Go out to dinner on Friday nights? Sleep in on Sundays?

It seemed an impossible dream.

She thought of his blue eyes, an ocean that pulled her under again and again, that made her believe it would be okay to let go and drown.

Except letting go was a mistake. Letting go meant losing herself the way her mother had lost herself time and time again. All the unspoken things between them were for the best, just like they were for the best with her mother.

Sometimes it was better to let sleeping dogs lie.

3

It was after ten in the morning by the time Ronan returned to the house. He and Nick had abandoned their post outside Moran's office after midnight when the congressman left. They'd followed him home, then abandoned that location when several hours passed without movement.

Ronan had been too wound up to go home. He'd dropped Nick at his car at the office and taken the elevator to MIS's headquarters on the fifth floor, running down the ways he could get a tap on the phones of Whitmore Club members like Moran.

It wouldn't be hard to tap one or two of them, but the club had twenty board members. Ronan needed to narrow the field.

Mark Reilly, their greeter-slash-security-detail,

wasn't yet at the office and Declan was undoubtedly still in bed with another Boston beauty. The whole place had the hushed air of a library, which suited Ronan's purposes just fine.

He'd spent the next three hours reviewing the details of Elise's case, going over every person of interest their investigation had uncovered, looking for stones that had not yet been turned.

When he'd been through all the data, he called Clay to check on the work his team was doing to uncover the owners behind the club in Dubai. Clay was still working, butting his digital head against seemingly impenetrable firewalls and security protocols that frustrated him every bit as much as it frustrated Ronan.

They'd never been able to track the home server of the Manifest site that had led Ronan and Julia to the Whitmore Club and Dubai. Whoever was structuring Manifest's digital security was better than good, something Clay took as a personal challenge.

Ronan had sat at his desk, his eyes pulled to the sea, a reflection of the lightening sky beyond his office's glass walls. Nick's words echoed in his mind, a warning: as much as Nick and Declan had come to care for Julia, they wouldn't sanction use of the company's resources on the Berenger case forever. Sometimes cutting your losses was good business, a fact even Ronan couldn't deny.

But he would not cut his losses on Julia's sister. Not until she was ready to do so, and that would never happen. By the time he left the office he was already planning how he could keep working the case without MIS, how he would hand off the company's leadership to Nick, bring in Reilly to work in the field, hire someone else to secure the front desk.

Theirs was a lucrative business. An invisible cash business. Ronan had plenty of money stashed. They all did, in part thanks to Nick's wise investments. Ronan would use every penny to find Elise on his own if that's what it came to, anything to ease the pain in Julia's eyes, to break down the last barrier she held between them.

It was the thought of her — at home in his bed, her eyes sleepy as she stretched, her fingers stroking Chief's fur as she woke up — that finally got him out of the office.

When he stepped into the kitchen, she was at the counter, a cup of coffee and the newspaper in front of her, Chief at her feet. He was surprised to see

Declan standing at the stove, cooking eggs and bacon.

Chief ran over, shoving her wet nose into Ronan's palm. "Hey, girl. Are you begging for food again?" He baby-talked to the dog. "Julia thinks I don't know she feeds you bacon but I do."

"I have no idea what you're talking about," Julia said. Was it his imagination that her eyes lit up when she saw him? Wishful thinking? "Long night?"

He nodded and leaned down to kiss her. "Long night." He looked at Declan, wondering if he'd already gotten rid of his one-night stand or if he'd had a rare night alone. "Losing your charm?"

"Very funny," Declan said, turning off the heat on the bacon. A lock of dark hair fell over his forehead, a cowlick from childhood that he'd never outgrown. "I'm not a rabbit, you know."

"Ew," Julia said without looking up from the paper.

"He's the one who brought it up," Declan said.

Ronan plucked a piece of bacon from the hot frying pan. "What's the occasion?"

Even as he asked, he knew the answer: it was her. Julia.

She had a way of drawing them all out, bringing

them together for baseball games in the living room and home-cooked meals in the kitchen.

Six months ago he would have said nothing was missing from the house. He'd lived with his brothers long enough that everything operated like a finely oiled machine. They each had their jobs and they each did them, except for Dec, who needed reminders.

Sometimes they'd ordered a pizza or had beers when they got home from the office, but they'd returned quickly to their own activities or respective wings of the house. Nick might have a date, the details of which he kept to himself with women that, like Ronan, he never brought home. Declan would be out prowling the city with his friends from college, looking to score a woman he wouldn't hesitate to bring back to the house.

Ronan's life was even less exciting — extra hours at the office or in the field, an occasional one-night stand at someone else's place, runs with Chief by the water.

Something had shifted since Julia had been staying with them. She was like a magnet, drawing them out from their corners, pulling them into her orbit with the smell of homemade cookies in the kitchen or reality TV in the living room, something she swore she hadn't watched before Elise went missing.

The shows were a source of entertainment for them all, causing them to shout and jeer at the TV like they were the World Series, pitting them against each other in their bets of who would cheat next, who would get a rose, who would be kicked out.

It was an escape for them all, not just the TV but the house that had become a refuge against everything ugly and painful. He saw it in the way Julia spent so much time there, leaving only to walk the beach with Ronan and Chief or visit her grandfather for their weekly dinners.

As a freelance network security specialist, she was uniquely qualified to analyze Clay's data, but she combed through it curled up on the couch with her laptop or sitting at the kitchen island, head bent to the screen, glasses sliding off her nose.

Ronan wanted it to last forever, wanted her to stay with him forever, and he often had to remind himself that the situation was a product of her tragedy, something that made him feel ashamed for the sheer joy her presence brought him.

Declan set a plate of bacon and eggs in front of Ronan and gestured to a paper bag on the counter. "Nick brought home bagels."

"He sleeping?" Ronan asked, sitting next to Julia and shoving a bite of eggs into his mouth.

"I assume so," Declan said.

"Did you have any luck last night?" Julia asked, her plate untouched in front of her.

Ronan shook his head. "Afraid not."

Her shoulders sagged. "I thought this round of names was going to get us somewhere."

It had taken them weeks to work through all the long-standing members of the Whitmore Club, weeks of surveilling homes and businesses and pied-à-terre.

Three weeks ago they'd reached the last ten board members on the list. After this they were out of leads unless Clay cracked the people behind Gold in Dubai, or even more unlikely, caught a break on the digging he was doing on the Darknet about Manifest's members.

"It's not over yet." Ronan was glad Nick wasn't in the kitchen to give him a meaningful glance. It would be an unpleasant reminder of their conversation in the car, and one Julia would more than likely notice. "All we need is one break."

She nodded, but he could see that she wasn't convinced.

He wanted to tell her not to worry, that he would

find the break they needed if it took him the rest of his life, that he would leave MIS if it came to it, travel to the ends of the earth, spend every last dime looking for her sister.

He was self-aware enough to know it was irrational. Worse than irrational: it was bad business, but in the Berenger case he'd found the perfect storm of psychological fuckery — a chance to save someone like Erin before it was too late and a chance to do it for the woman who made him realize he'd been a fool to think he'd ever been in love before.

"I'm going to get ready for work," Declan said.

Ronan covered his heart with his hand, feigning shock. "I don't believe my ears."

"Don't get excited," Declan said, heading for the hall that would take him to his wing of the house. "I have a date with the hottest blond I've ever seen tonight. Don't expect me in at all tomorrow."

"Thanks for breakfast," Julia called after him.

Ronan stared at her, a smile creeping onto the corners of his mouth.

"What?" she asked.

He shook his head. "What kind of magic are you working here?"

"What do you mean?"

"Dec's making breakfast, going into the office. What's next? Monogamy?"

She laughed. "You give me too much credit. Monogamy for Declan is way above my pay grade."

He took her hand and pulled her onto his lap. Not wanting to spook her, he chose his words carefully, mindful of the way she skirted any talk of their future like an animal steering clear of predatory territory, the way she held something back even when she told him she loved him, even when they were naked and intertwined.

"I like having you here," he said. "Nick and Dec like having you here too."

She smiled. "Thanks for letting me stay while I sort things out."

He swallowed against the implication — that it was temporary, a product of Elise's disappearance, of the memories dredged up by the apartment she and Elise had shared.

"You can stay as long as you want," he said.

Stay forever. Never leave my side.

She touched her lips to his, pressing against him until his cock jumped to life in his jeans. Her mouth was soft and yielding, her hands trailing his chest, but he couldn't shake the feeling that it was all a distraction — another way to avoid a discussion about the future.

He knew what was between them was real. He felt it in the way her body melted into his like mercury, the way the boundaries between them fell when he was inside her.

So why did it feel so tenuous?

4

Julia waited to slip from the bed until Ronan's breathing was slow and regular beside her. His arm was heavy across her body as she eased carefully out from under it, cursing the fact that she couldn't sleep, that the one night she'd gotten him to hand off the stakeout at Moran's to Nick, she couldn't even settle in and enjoy it.

She looked down at him as she slipped his T-shirt over her naked body. His arm was still flung across the mattress where she'd been a moment before, his expression serene. His thick hair was tousled from their lovemaking and she felt a rush of fresh desire as she remembered his mouth on her skin, his fingers and cock inside her.

Her lust for him still took her by surprise, the barrier she erected between them harder to maintain as he brought her to orgasm over and over again, as he probed her body like an eager explorer determined to leave no territory unmapped.

She considered laying back down, waking him with her mouth and hands, giving herself over to physical sensation again in the hopes that it would eventually lead to sleep.

She discarded the idea. Ronan spent most of every night holed up in his car, staring through the binoculars at their latest stakeout target in an effort to find a new clue that would lead them to Elise. It wasn't fair to wake him just to keep herself distracted on the one night when he had a shot at decent rest.

Chief lifted her head from her bed on the floor and Julia raised a hand. Ronan had taught her that the signal meant Stay, and the dog whimpered and lowered her head back to the cushion as Julia left the room.

Her bare feet moved silently across the runner in the hall. She liked everything about the house — its rambling floor plan that was separated into private wings for each of the Murphy brothers, the communal living and kitchen areas that guaranteed she was never alone for long, the quiet of it at night.

Declan was usually out in the early part of the evening, but he almost always returned home to sleep, albeit with one of his conquests, and Nick was more often than not at home when he wasn't at the office or playing rugby with the intramural team that seemed to be his primary source of activity.

Julia was comforted by the comings and goings of the three brothers, by their familiarity with each other. It reminded her of Elise, of the unique sibling bond that was familiarity and acceptance and just enough baggage to keep things interesting.

She took a seat at the end of the sofa and folded her legs under her body. It was hard to believe it had been four months since she'd first walked into the house, scraped up from her run-in with Ronan in the alley behind Seth Campbell's brownstone, having no idea that her gramps had hired MIS to find Elise, having no idea that she would come to love the man with deep-sea eyes who had so tenderly dressed her wounded leg.

She'd fallen for him hard and fast. Too hard and fast, as evidenced by the fact that she'd been back in his arms shortly after the debacle in Dubai.

She hadn't been able to look at him on the plane home, hadn't been able to see anything but Gold, the long hallway of closed doors, an image of her sister behind one of them, waiting for Julia to save her.

But the anger had left her body as soon as Ronan

dropped her at the apartment, his face a mask of restrained pain and regret.

In the cast of her family, Julia had always played the starring role of Doer of Things That Must Be Done. It wasn't always appreciated, but she knew too well that someone had to do those things.

Someone had to say no when saying yes was easier. Someone had to save the money and pay the bills and keep the boat on an even keel when everyone else seemed determined to sink it.

Plus, she'd missed him. Had missed him with a fierceness she'd been afraid to examine too closely. When he'd appeared at her door with another apology — an apology for carrying her screaming from Gold, saving her life when she'd reached the point where she didn't care about it at all, when saving Elise was all that mattered — she hadn't even hesitated before letting him in.

She sighed, reaching for her laptop and forcing herself from the past.

Forcing herself from the future.

She didn't know what would happen between her and Ronan long-term. She only knew that she loved him, that she was scared of how much she loved him.

She opened her laptop and the screen came to

life, the browser still open to the page for Manifest, the dark blue door glowing like a mirage.

It had opened only once for her — when it had revealed the logo for Gold behind the stylized "M" that they now knew stood for Manifest. She had no idea why the people behind Manifest had invited her to one of their lairs after she'd been caught snooping at the Whitmore Club. She could only assume it was because she hadn't been working with Ronan at the time, not formally anyway.

Had they thought she would come alone? Had they planned to take her like they'd taken her sister? Shut her up, keep her from asking questions, sell her to one of their clients on the Darknet as a bonus?

She didn't like to think about it, about what could have happened if Ronan hadn't been there to haul her out of the club. Maybe that's why she'd forgiven him so easily. Maybe she knew deep down she would have disappeared into the black hole of money and corruption that had swallowed her sister.

Maybe she valued her own life more than she was willing to admit.

She swallowed her guilt at the thought. She would do anything to save Elise.

Anything.

She clicked on the blue door and was unsurprised when nothing happened. She'd tried more times than she could count, hoping for another invitation, entertaining the thought of accepting it without telling Ronan if it came, wondering if the only way she would know what had happened to Elise was to let it happen to her too.

5

Ronan watched the office building through the windshield, his eyes on the lights coming from the fourth floor. It was Congressman Moran's floor, and Ronan knew he was still up there because he'd followed Moran back to the office after a meeting at the Alibi Lounge inside the Liberty Hotel.

They'd had Moran's daily schedule for the past two weeks thanks to Clay, who had a long and storied history of hacking calendars to help MIS on the job in spite of his assertion that it was beneath him.

The people behind the Manifest website were more worthy opponents, which was probably why Clay was still trying to hack his way in even though Ronan had given up the angle.

It was almost eleven p.m. but Moran's car hadn't

left the parking garage since his return from the meeting at Alibi. Ronan had to give him credit: whatever else he was or wasn't, the man worked long hours.

Ronan thought about Moran's wife, a WASPy blond nicknamed Mouse. They had three kids — two sons and a daughter — all of whom attended Groton Prep. Mouse was from an old-money family with an inheritance that kept the family flush in spite of Moran's congressional paycheck. They lived in an understated but valuable home in Beacon Hill, gave to all the right charities, and attended all the right events.

Ronan had seen plenty while staking out the board members of the Whitmore Club — affairs of every variety, prostitutes, kink clubs, and one particularly sad and quite large Senator who's greatest vice was stopping at the Mobil gas station on his way home and stocking up on an assortment of junk food which he ate breathtakingly fast in his car, after which he wept over his steering wheel before finishing the drive home.

It was the only time Ronan could ever recall feeling guilty observing someone as part of a job.

Not all of the Whitmore board members had secrets — at least not that Ronan had uncovered. So far Moran fell into the category of those members who went to work, had an occasional long lunch, and sometimes stopped at their kid's Little League game on the way home.

Were they all really upstanding citizens who also happened to be in seats of power at one of the clubs whose logos had appeared on the one page of Manifest's website that Clay had been able to access?

Or were they just careful?

Ronan thought about Julia, about the way he'd woken up the night before to find her gone, her face lit by the glow of her laptop when he'd come upon her on the sofa in the living room.

She didn't want him to know she was still stalking Manifest's website, one of many secrets he knew she kept from him. He didn't push. He had a feeling Julia had been holding things close to the vest for a long time, each of her secrets a piece of the Jenga puzzle that would come crashing down if she started examining them — or worse, talking about them.

She would talk when she was ready. In the meantime, he savored the times when they were in bed, the closest she came to giving herself over fully to him. It wasn't total surrender. He still felt the missing part of her — the part she kept locked away in the innermost vault of her heart — like an almost invisible piece of a complicated puzzle.

He wondered how many people had settled for this much from her in the past. How many people had told themselves they were getting all of her.

He pushed aside the thought. He and Julia didn't talk about their former lovers, and he had no desire to think about her in the arms of another man.

He straightened in the driver's seat of his silver Audi as a limo pulled up like a long shadow in front of Moran's building.

He reached for the binoculars on the passenger seat without taking his eyes off the entrance of the office building.

The limo idled for almost five minutes before the office doors opened and Connor Moran stepped onto the sidewalk.

He kept his head down as he strode toward the limo, slipping into the backseat so quickly Ronan might have missed the whole thing if he hadn't been paying attention.

"Siri, call Clay," Ronan said, still watching the limo through the binoculars.

"What's up?" Clay asked by way of a greeting.

"You still have access to the DMV?" Ronan asked without identifying himself.

Clay snorted. "That's like asking if I have access to Netflix."

"I'm going to have a plate for you in a second. I need you to run it and give me everything you can find," Ronan said.

"You're the boss."

6

Julia watched as Ronan taped a picture to the ever-evolving board of Whitmore Club members and their associates. They had a flow chart in the digital case file of Elise's disappearance, something Julia had insisted she be given access to, but they kept the hard copies on the big board in the MIS conference room. It was easier to make connections when it was all laid out in front of you, when you could see how people were connected and how they weren't.

Ronan had taped the new photo at the end of a red line drawn from Congressman Moran's name and photo.

"Davis Porter," Ronan said. "If he looks familiar, it's because he's the current head of the Federal Reserve."

The man in the photo was at least sixty with silver hair, a long nose, and angular features.

"That's who the limo belongs to?" Nick asked.

They were standing around the conference table, all of them too amped to sit.

"Not outright, but that's where it leads. The car is currently requisitioned to his driver, and Porter has been spotted entering and exiting it on several occasions since I spotted it outside of Moran's office."

"What the fuck…?" Declan said.

Julia wondered if he was rubbing his temples because of the strange and unexpected break in Elise's case or because of the brunette Julia had spotted leaving the house carrying her shoes that morning just after sunrise.

"He's not on the roster of Whitmore Club members," Nick said.

Ronan nodded. "Correct."

"Then how do we know this ties into Elise's disappearance?" Nick asked.

Julia was gratified to hear him use Elise's name. It sounded personal, like she was real to Nick. Like he cared about her.

Ronan sighed. "We don't. Not technically. But there are some… oddities associated with Porter as they relate to some of the Whitmore board members."

"What kind of oddities?" Julia asked.

Ronan shrugged. "A few dinner meetings, some overlapping acquaintances, things that wouldn't necessarily be unusual — except for one thing."

"Do you want us to guess?" Nick said.

Ronan turned to the board and taped another piece of paper to it under Davis Porter's picture.

Julia looked at the picture, an aerial shot of a massive stone building surrounded by trees, and in the distance, some kind of dome. "What is it?"

"It's a private residence in Firenze, Italy, just outside Florence." Ronan picked up the red marker and started drawing lines from some of the Whitmore members to the picture of the villa. She recognized the names, ticking them off as he drew the lines, starting with Davis Porter. "All of these men flew into Florence on March 21st. They all left the next day."

"But Porter isn't a member of the Whitmore Club," Julia said, trying to figure out what Ronan was getting at.

"No, but when Moran got into his car I thought about Dubai, and about the page on Manifest's website that seemed to be advertising meeting locations. I had Clay pull everything they could find on Porter, including his travel over the past six months. Then I cross-referenced it against the travel of the Whitmore board members to see if a number of them had been at the same place at the same time."

"And you came up with Florence," Nick said.

"I came up with Florence."

"Who owns the villa?" Declan asked.

Julia wasn't surprised to see that his eyes were suddenly sharp. When she'd first met him, she'd assumed he was the family fuck-up. Almost every big family had one.

But Declan had proven her wrong. He could make connections hungover and sleep-deprived that eluded her at her best. It was a mistake to underestimate him.

"That's the other thing." Ronan said. "Ownership of the villa looks a lot like ownership of the Manifest website."

Nick looked at Ronan. "Impossible to trace?"

Ronan nodded. "Shell companies, empty IDs, you name it."

Nick walked to the wall, his gaze traveling over the photographs and the intersecting lines. "Anyone think of any reason why all these guys — all these rich, powerful guys — would converge on Florence at the same time? Some kind of financial or political conference? Anything?"

"I had Clay run it," Ronan said. "It was midweek, and the only big conference in town was fashion-related." He hesitated. "But once I made the connection, I had Clay run travel records for Davis and the Whitmore members going back two years, just to see if there had ever been another time when they all went to the same city at the same time."

"And?" Julia felt like she was going to jump out of her skin.

"And several of them have made repeat trips to Florence, always on the last Saturday of every month," Ronan said.

"The last Saturday of every month," Nick repeated. "The same members every month?"

Ronan shook his head. "It varies, but it's definitely the same core group."

"What are you thinking?" Declan asked.

"I'm thinking these guys are all members of Manifest and the villa in Florence is home base for monthly parties," Ronan said. "I'm thinking they can't all make it all the time, but they get away when they can."

Julia's stomach turned over. "What kind of parties?"

Sympathy shadowed his eyes when he looked at her. "Your guess is as good as mine, although I'm sure we're guessing the same kinds of things."

Julia grabbed onto the back of one of the conference chairs as if that would help to steady her. Like that would stop the wave of nausea that threatened to overtake her. Like that would stop her from imagining Elise at the mercy of a bunch of rich assholes who thought they'd earned the right to use her against her will.

"I'd be surprised if the Whitmore members we've already tagged represent all of Manifest's membership." Julia was glad that Ronan continued, that he didn't wait for her to say anything more. She didn't trust herself to speak without screaming. "Clay's working on getting into ENAV's database so we can run numbers on repeat visitors to Florence on or around the last Saturday of the month. That might clue us in to other members of Manifest, but it might take a while."

"ENAV?" Julia repeated.

"It's like the TSA in Italy," Declan explained. "They have customs records on anyone entering the country via its airspace."

"Helicopters too?" Julia asked.

"Good point," Ronan said. "The members who

live closer to Florence might come in via chopper. We'll pull flight records from private heliports in the area too."

Julia nodded. "How long is a while?"

"Weeks, maybe months," he admitted.

It didn't surprise her that he knew she was talking about Clay. Their communication had been like this from the beginning: easy, seamless, synchronized.

"We can't wait that long," Julia said.

He nodded slowly. And now his eyes were shaded with something deeper than regret. Something that looked a lot like fear. "I know."

The vise that had been gripping her chest since Ronan mentioned the parties in Florence began to ease. Now at least they could do something. "When do we leave?"

7

Even before he and Julia hit the porch of the house, Ronan heard his father's voice. The words were indistinct, but Ronan would know the deep timbre, low and commanding, of his father's voice anywhere.

Julia cast him a questioning look as they approached the house through the courtyard.

"My father," Ronan said.

She lifted her eyebrows. In the three months she'd been living at the house, she'd never had occasion to meet Thomas Murphy. It hadn't been intentional but Ronan wasn't willing to swear it hadn't been the work of his subconscious.

Despite his truce with his father, there was undoubtedly baggage in their relationship, and Ronan wasn't eager to explain it to Julia when they were already standing on the shifting sand of Elise's disappearance.

Nick was in almost daily contact with their father, but Ronan had somehow managed to be busy anytime Nick or Declan went over to the house in South Boston, an area that had been rough when Thomas Murphy bought the row house with Ronan's mother back in 1982 but which had become gentrified in the last decade.

"Is it okay that I'm here?" Julia asked as they approached the door.

Ronan reached for her hand. "It's more than okay."

They'd stayed at the office after Nick and Declan left, Ronan immersing himself in a conversation with Clay about what it would take to gain him access to the next Manifest event in Florence, and Julia combing through the background on the members of the Whitmore Club that they could now be almost certain were part of Manifest.

Ronan had no desire to address the white elephant of the trip to Florence — whether Julia would go, if she did go what her role would be — and he'd been relieved that she was willing to leave it for another time.

It was only a reprieve but he would take it.

Their father's voice grew louder as they opened the door that opened onto the kitchen.

"... that back window that's been sticking for the past six months..." His voice trailed off as Ronan and Julia stepped into the kitchen.

"Well, look what the cat dragged in," his father said, looking him up and down. His gaze shifted to Julia as he got off the stool at the island and walked toward them. "You must be Julia."

She smiled and held out her hand. "It's nice to meet you."

Ronan tried not to think about how their father knew Julia's name, about what had been said between Nick and their father — Declan was nowhere to be found — before Ronan and Julia showed up.

"The pleasure is all mine," Ronan's dad said. His voice was genial, but Ronan could feel his cop's brain turning, could feel him compiling impressions about Julia to review later. "I might have met you earlier if my son didn't like to pretend he was an orphan."

Julia shifted uncomfortably on her feet. "Oh, I'm sure it's not that. He's been so busy..."

"Dad, stop," Ronan said.

His dad shrugged and returned to the island

where a beer was sweating on the granite countertop. Chief was sitting next to his stool, her tail wagging like a windshield wiper on the floor. She'd always been fond of Ronan's dad.

Nick handed Ronan a beer without comment, for which Ronan was grateful.

"You want?" Nick asked Julia, tipping his head at the beer.

"I think I'll go change," she said.

Ronan looked at her. "Stay."

"You sure?"

She obviously didn't know what to make of the visit from Thomas Murphy, and Ronan had no way of telling her that the tension in the air had nothing to do with her and everything to do with the stories that had been written in the Murphy history book long before she arrived on the scene. That it had to do with the death of Erin and even their mother, that it had to do with the fact that their sister, Nora, hardly ever came home anymore, that Thomas Murphy's sons had declined to follow in his footsteps as servants of the law and had instead formed a company whose sole purpose was to subvert it.

"I'm sure," Ronan said.

"You want to rethink that beer?" Nick's shit-eating grin spoke loud and clear: welcome to our nightmare.

"Um, sure. Okay." She slid onto a stool across from Ronan's dad.

Nick pulled another beer from the fridge, uncapped it, and handed it to her.

"How have you been, Pops?" Ronan studied his father's face, relieved to see that he looked healthy, his broad face tan from the time he spent on his boat in the bay, his silver hair still thick and full.

"Right as rain," his dad said. His shoulders were still broad under a navy windbreaker, although a slight paunch had grown in his midsection.

"What have you been up to?" Ronan asked, trying to keep the conversation in trouble-free territory.

"Oh, you know, this and that." His dad took a swig of the beer. "That old house always needs something. Between that and the boat and the guys, I keep busy enough."

The guys were his dad's friends from BPD, most of them retired like him.

"Glad to hear it," Ronan said. "You look good."

His dad scowled. "Why wouldn't I look good. I'm only sixty-eight, for god's sake."

Ronan shrugged. "I'm just saying. It's a compliment."

He stifled a sigh. It had been like this with his dad for as long as he could remember, the two of them tiptoeing around each other until something stupid set one of them off.

Had it started after Ronan's mother died? He'd been close to his mother before her death, preferring her easy company to the bristle and expectations of his dad. It was true that Ronan had met those expectations in spades before starting MIS. Quarterback of the football team, captain of Debate Club, Honors Student, Soldier.

He'd molded himself to his dad's image of the ideal firstborn son, and while Ronan didn't remember resenting it until after Erin's death, he did remember being aware of the expectations.

There had been none of that with his mother. She'd been easy with her love, her big laugh and warm green eyes the sandpaper that smoothed out his dad's rough edges.

"Dad's thinking of replacing the windows in the house," Nick volunteered.

Ronan both resented Nick's relationship with their dad and was relieved that it took the heat off of him. He had no idea how their relationship had survived Nick's defection from the BPD. He'd been the good son by then, the one who'd been willing to follow their dad onto the police force, wear the uniform, move up the ranks.

Like so many things, that had ended with Erin's death, but somehow Nick's relationship with their dad had survived.

"Sounds like a good idea," Ronan said.

What the fuck was going on? Why was his dad here making small talk about home repair? This wasn't the first time months had gone by between Ronan's visits to the house in Southie.

"Nick tells me you're going to Italy."

Ronan had to force himself not to glare at Nick. "That's right."

His dad turned his beer bottle in his hand. There were a million questions in his silence. A million things already said. A million more they would never dare speak.

He looked up and met Ronan's eyes. "How long will you be gone?"

"Hard to say."

In the pause that followed Ronan thought about all the arguments they'd had in the past about MIS, each one carefully clothed in generic language that made it impossible to know how much his dad knew about their business, that made it impossible not to realize he knew enough.

Ronan had tried explaining to his dad why they'd founded MIS, how they'd had to do something tangible in the wake of Erin's death and the court's decision to set free the dealer who had introduced her to heroin.

It had been pointless. Their dad's view of honor was specific and unmovable, reliant on laws and codes that Ronan no longer believed in, that he hadn't believed in in a long time.

"You'll be careful," his dad finally said.

Ronan nodded.

His dad slid off the stool and bent to scratch Chief's head. "Maybe when you get back we'll take the boat out. You and Nick and Dec, and Finn, if he ever shows his face again. Maybe we can even get Nora to come home." His dad looked at Julia. "You'll come too, Julia. We'll pack beers and fishing poles."

Julia smiled. "Sounds perfect."

Ronan's throat tightened with something like guilt. Something like love.

His dad would never admit to being lonely, but Ronan saw that he was.

"I'd like that," Ronan said.

Maybe this time it would happen. Maybe they

wouldn't make excuses about how busy they were or how they were going to be out of town. Maybe they would set aside the past and all their differences.

That they'd once been father and son and there had been love.

Ronan was surprised to realize he hoped it was still true.

8

Julia was still thinking about Ronan's dad when they walked Chief on the beach that night. The sun was just beginning to sink behind the city, the air still balmy, a gentle breeze blowing in off the water. They walked slowly at the water line, carrying their shoes while Chief trotted ahead, nose to the ground.

Julia had had no preconceived notions about Thomas Murphy. Ronan rarely spoke about him, and when he did she'd sensed a minefield she was hesitant to test. She had her own secrets, her own baggage, and she was happy to honor the unspoken agreement that seemed to exist between her and Ronan even if it meant some question marks.

But it was obvious Thomas Murphy loved his sons — all of them. She'd seen that much in the way he'd looked at Ronan and Nick, in his eagerness to spend time with them and the concern in his eyes when he'd mentioned Italy.

"Something you want to ask me?" Ronan said beside her.

She looked up at him. "Does he know? Your dad?"

"About the business?" Ronan asked.

She nodded.

His face was grim, his jaw set as he kept his eyes on the sand in front of them. "More or less."

"More or less?"

"It's not something we talk openly about," he said. "But he knows."

"I take it he doesn't approve?" she asked.

He laughed a little but there was no humor in it. "You could say that."

"Because he was a cop?"

"Probably," Ronan said. "Or maybe he was a cop because he doesn't approve."

"He's a law and order kind of guy?" she asked.

"He believes in rules."

She hesitated, not wanting to overstep. "Even after what happened to Erin?" It felt wrong to speak her name. Julia had the feeling it was sacred. She didn't know if she had the right.

"Even then," Ronan said. He bent to pick up a

stick in the sand and threw it into the shallow surf for Chief, who bounded after it. "It was hard for me to understand, the way he could just let it go."

Julia opened her mouth to say something, then changed her mind.

"What?" Ronan prodded.

"I was just going to say that I'm sure it wasn't easy," Julia said. "People are so different, the way they deal with things."

"Like you and Elise?" Ronan asked.

She turned her eyes to the sea, shimmering darkly in the distance as the sun sank below Boston's skyscrapers. She hadn't expected her questions about Ronan's father to be turned back on her but fair was fair.

"Our mom was kind of MIA growing up." Julia laughed, trying to make light of it, but it rang false even to her own ears. "Married and divorced four times. I learned to take care of things, to take care of Elise."

"And Elise?" he asked.

Chief brought the stick back and nosed Julia's hand. She took it from the dog's mouth and tossed it back into the water.

"Elise learned to let me take care of her. But

then, I'm guessing you already knew all that," she said.

"Reading about someone in a dossier isn't the same as knowing them. I never forget that." Chief had found something in the seaweed lining the shore. She bent her to investigate, burrowing into the kelp. Ronan gestured to a place just beyond the reach of the waves rolling ashore. "Want to sit?"

Julia lowered herself to the sand and hugged her knees to her chest. Chief was still nosing her way through the seaweed, the stick forgotten.

It had been strangely intimate, meeting Ronan's father, being privy to all the unspoken things that existed in families like his.

Like hers.

What would Ronan think if he were around Julia in her mother's company? Would he see what she saw — her mother negligent and self-absorbed? Or would he see what Julia had seen in Thomas Murphy: a human being who had made mistakes, but one who cared?

It was impossible to imagine. Julia hadn't seen her mother in over a year. Even she didn't know what it would be like.

"Were things... normal with your dad before Erin's death? Before your mom died?" Ronan had told her about his mother's death, his face a mask that made it clear it wasn't something he wanted to discuss or even remember. She imagined long illnesses like cancer did that to people.

Ronan's eyes were trained on the horizon. "It's hard to know if I'm remembering it right, but I think so. My mom was..." He exhaled. "She was great. Warm. Loving. Fun. I always wanted to please my dad, but I think that's to be expected. I don't remember behind unhappy though."

"I'm glad you have that," Julia said. "Those memories."

She wondered if it was harder to have something good and have it taken from you or if it was worse to never have it at all.

She felt his gaze on her face. "There must be good things from your childhood."

A series of images played across Julia's mind: she and Elise jumping on the bed and laughing until they fell in a heap on the covers, chasing each other around the kitchen with a whipped cream can, both of them shrieking, hiding under a blanket fort in the living room when they were in high school, giggling about Julia's first kiss.

"There are," she admitted. "I know I was lucky in a lot of ways. I had my gramps, and I had Elise."

But a voice had begun to whisper in her ear, a voice that said she wasn't being fair.

That she wasn't being honest.

Her mom had been there in the background, yelling at Julia and Elise to get off the bed, plucking the whipped cream can from Julia's hand and turning it on Elise with a laugh, trying to push her way into their blanket fort.

It wasn't everything but it wasn't nothing either.

Chief returned from her investigation of the seaweed and lay down next to Julia smelling like salt and wet fur.

"You know I'm going to Italy," she said.

She didn't want to talk about her mom anymore.

He didn't look at her. "What if I told you it was dangerous, not just for you but for me too?"

"How so?" she asked, taking in the line of his mouth, the set of his jaw in profile.

"I won't be able to think straight with you there," he said.

"I don't believe that. You're a professional. I'm sure you've worked under worse circumstances."

He turned to look at her, his blue eyes on fire. "Not like this, Julia."

Her chest tightened and she drew in a breath as she looked away. Saying I love you was easy compared to the current of emotion that ran through her when he looked at her like that.

She worked to keep her voice steady as she drew in the sand with her finger. "I'm not saying I have to go with you to the party." They hadn't even figured out yet how to get in, but it was a given that at least one of them would have to gain access to find out if Elise was there. "But I can't stay in Boston while you go to Italy to look for my sister. It will kill me."

For a long moment, he didn't speak, and she thought maybe she'd made her point.

"What if I said no?"

She looked up at him, anger flaring in her chest. "I'd like to go with you, to help however I can, even if it's just as backup for Clay's work. If you don't want me to go, I'll go alone, and I'm betting I'll have an easier time getting into that party than you will."

He glared at her. "That would be a suicide mission."

She shrugged. "Maybe, maybe not. But I'm not leaving my sister again, and I'm not sitting on my ass in Boston while you go to Italy looking for her."

He turned his eyes back to the water and cursed under his breath. "You're going to get yourself killed, but maybe that's the point."

"What's that supposed to mean? You think I have a death wish?"

He shook his head. "I don't know, Julia. Your grandfather hired us to find Elise so you wouldn't have to put yourself at risk. So why do you insist on doing it anyway?"

She swallowed the lump that rose in her throat. She didn't have an answer to his question. Maybe it was because she had so little to call her own that saving Elise gave her a sense of purpose. Or maybe she liked being Elise's savior more than she'd let on all those years when she played the martyr.

She pushed it all away. It wasn't that complicated.

"I left her behind in Dubai." He opened his mouth to say something and she hurried to continue before he could say anything. "I know I didn't have a choice, but I left her there. That's the truth. I've been looking out for her my whole life. I can't just turn that off. She's my sister."

When he turned to look at her the anguish on his face took her breath away. "Do you know how hard it's going to be for me to have you anywhere near those animals?"

She did. She saw it in his eyes.

She reached for his hand. "I do, and I'm sorry.

I'm just asking you to weigh that against how hard it would be for me to stay."

He looked at her for a long moment before pulling her against him. "Dammit, Julia."

She leaned into his warmth and felt no victory in the fact that she'd won.

9

Ronan sat in the back booth of an Applebee's and watched as the man entered the restaurant. He looked around, peering through the dimly lit space until his gaze landed on Ronan, then started toward him.

It had been nearly a year since Ronan had seen Braden Kane. Ronan had been on a layover in L.A. on his way back from a job in Australia and had called Nora to see if she wanted to meet for dinner.

He hadn't been surprised when she'd shown up with Braden. He and Nora had worked together at the FBI before they'd left to join forces with Locke Montgomery, who ran an outfit with the same goals as MIS, if not with the same rules.

MIS was a business, and it was run like one.

Risks were weighed and calculated, the quickest, least risky path to completion taken.

As with MIS, Locke's enterprise was about more than money. Unlike MIS, it was equal parts a way for Montgomery to push the envelope, and Ronan tried not to think about Nora and Braden working for someone who seemed to relish risk where MIS avoided it.

Ronan had met Montgomery only once and had had to hide his surprise: the man looked more Zen surfer than ruthless vigilante, but he'd learned in the years that Nora worked with him that Montgomery had his own brand of justice.

"Hey," Braden said, folding his large frame into the seat across from Ronan.

"Hey. How long do you have?" Ronan asked. Braden had been in Boston on a job and was due to fly out later that night.

"About an hour," Braden said. His hair was still cut short in a typical Fed haircut even though it had been years since he'd been part of the Bureau.

Ronan understood. Old habits die hard.

They ordered beers from a waiter who looked too young to drink them. Ronan waited until he was out of earshot to speak.

"How's my sister?"

"She's good," Braden said. He chuckled and his face was transformed. "Keeps me on my toes."

"I'd expect nothing less." Ronan liked Braden, but it was always weird to sit across from the guy who was sleeping with his sister, even when that sister was pushing thirty.

They were quiet as the waiter dropped off their beers. You could never be too careful in public places.

"I take it you're in some deep shit," Braden said when the waiter was out of earshot.

Ronan grinned. "Am I?"

He'd used a secure communication channel to give Braden the broad strokes of Elise Berenger's disappearance and the connection to Manifest, hoping Braden's connections with both Locke Montgomery and the Bureau might provide intel that would give them a leg up in Florence.

"Word is to steer clear of these guys," Braden said.

"Manifest?"

Braden nodded.

"Whose word?" Ronan asked.

"Everyone's. Guys at the Bureau, some of the guys at FVEY…"

Ronan tried to hide his surprise. FVEY stood for

Five Eyes, five countries — Canada, Australia, New Zealand, the UK, and the US — who shared top secret intelligence with each other.

"Are you serious?"

"As a heart attack," Braden said.

"And they're going along? Steering clear?"

"Officially," Braden said.

It didn't bode well. If FVEY was willing to look the other way on Manifest's crimes, it meant the players were even bigger than Ronan anticipated.

"And unofficially?"

"There's a joint task force working quietly. It's small, tight-knit to avoid leaks," Braden said.

"Did they know anything about Florence?"

Braden looked into his beer like he would find the words he was searching for in the foam at the top of the glass. "Nothing definitive, but there is some chatter."

"I'm listening."

Braden looked around, like the subject matter made him paranoid. "Word on the Darknet is that they're bringing in a fresh batch of girls this month. Rumor has it it's a showcase, a place to give the girls a test run before an auction that's supposed to take place next month."

Showcase... auction...

Ronan forced himself to ignore the fact that they were talking about women, about human beings, about Julia's sister.

"And all the girls will be there? In Florence?" Ronan asked.

"I don't have anything but what I told you," Braden said.

"Location of the auction?" Ronan could hardly get the words out.

"Sorry." Braden shook his head. "I don't know why I'm still surprised there are heartless bastards in the world."

Ronan shrugged. "I don't know either."

He wasn't surprised in the least. It was why he was able to do what he did, why he was able to kill without the impediment of his conscience. Living among one's fellow man implied a certain moral contract — namely not to enslave, torture, or murder them.

If someone couldn't abide by that contract, they had to be eliminated. In a perfect world, those people would be eliminated before they could poison the rest of society. Barring that, Ronan was more than happy to serve once they'd proven themselves a danger to everyone else.

"So I take it you're heading to Florence?" Braden asked.

He said it like he said everything, with a calm that made Ronan wonder if he ever lost his cool. It was one of the things Ronan liked about Kane, one of the reasons he was okay with Kane being with his sister: he might work for Montgomery, but Braden was as unruffled as still water.

Ronan had done background on him when he'd first found out he was seeing Nora and had discovered a decorated FBI agent who'd spearheaded the takedown of one of the world's most notorious mob bosses.

Of course, that mob boss was replaced by another, but the new one was easier for the Feds to work with, and sometimes that was as good as it got.

Ronan took a drink of his beer. "You got it."

"How can I help?" Braden asked.

"I need to get into the next party," Ronan said.

"What's the invite look like?"

"Don't know."

Braden chuckled and shook his head. "Want us to do the job for you too?"

"Don't be a prick," Ronan said. "I've got my guys on it, but the next party is two weeks from Saturday, and I need all hands on deck in case my team doesn't crack it, especially if your intel is accurate. I have a feeling it's not going to be an engraved invitation, if you catch my meaning."

Braden lifted his eyebrows. "Digital?"

"Just a guess," Ronan said. "But their website is tighter than Fort Knox. My guy hasn't been able to get in, and he's been working on it for three months."

"Maybe your guy sucks," Braden said.

"He's a former NSA lead analyst with expertise in cybercrime and digital terrorism."

Braden raised his glass. "Touché."

"Based on that and on what we've seen elsewhere, Manifest is a high-tech operation. I'd be surprised if the invite was a piece of paper," Ronan said.

"So you need us to figure out what it is and then get you in?"

Ronan nodded. "I figured you've still got connections at the Bureau."

"I do."

"Good." Ronan looked at the beer in his hand, his thoughts turning to Julia. He couldn't afford to make mistakes, not with her insistence on coming to Florence. "We need a break."

Braden tossed back the rest of his beer. "Oh man... You are in the shit."

Ronan looked at him. "What are you talking about?"

"You're doing this for a woman."

Ronan couldn't hide his annoyance. "We have a client."

"Maybe," Braden said. "But there's a woman involved somehow."

"How do you know?"

"Because I've seen that look on your face — in the mirror, when I was fighting with myself over the Sokolov case."

It was the case that had prompted Braden to leave the FBI, the case that had turned Braden Kane and Ronan's sister from friends to lovers. Nora had followed Braden to Montgomery's organization not long after a close friend at the Bureau had turned out to be a mole.

"She's the victim's sister," Ronan admitted. No point being coy.

"Sounds complicated."

"You don't know the half of it," Ronan said.

Braden met his eyes. "If you know your sister, you know I do."

He had a point. Nora had the Murphy stubbornness — not to mention the Murphy temper — in spades. It hadn't been an easy road for her and Braden, from working with the Feds to going rogue with Locke Montgomery. Nora was a trained agent, every bit as good as Kane and anyone else at the FBI. It made her a powerful ally when Braden had his back against the wall, but Ronan was learning that it was hard to protect someone who didn't want or even need your protection.

"How did you reconcile it?" Ronan asked.

Braden studied him. "I didn't. I love her. What am I going to do? Ask her to be somebody different?"

10

Julia walked into the flat and looked around, rendered speechless. When Ronan had said they would stay in an apartment in Florence, she'd expected a charming little place with cracks in the walls and peeling wallpaper.

This was not a place with cracks in the walls and peeling wallpaper.

Ronan took their bags into another room while Julia looked up at the soaring ceilings, intricate frescos painted between deep moldings that separated the ceiling into four different panels.

The sunlight making its way into the room from the big windows cast the pale aqua walls in a soft light, making them shimmer like the shallow waters of the Caribbean.

She peered around the heavy linen draperies to

the Arno river, snaking its way through the city just a few hundred feet from the apartment, and reached for the brass fitting on the big multi-paned window. It opened outward and a breeze caressed her shoulders on its way into the room.

"Will it do?"

She turned to find Ronan looking at her with an expression she couldn't define. "This belongs to MIS?"

"Technically, it belongs to me," Ronan said. "But it's really Nick's doing."

"Nick?"

She and Ronan had flown alone on the company jet to get settled in Florence while Nick and Declan wrapped up things at home and the office. After they took Chief to stay with a friend of Ronan's from the Navy, they would join Ronan and Julia in Florence — along with Clay — to start planning a way into Manifest's next party.

"I let him manage my money," Ronan said. "I don't have the patience for it — or the interest."

"And he bought this place for you?" She was still getting her head around the scope of MIS's business, both the work they did and the money they brought in.

"He advised me to buy it."

She tore her eyes from his, taking in the designer furnishings mixed with antiques that somehow looked both timeworn and fresh. She hadn't seen the other rooms yet, but she had the sense that the apartment was large, that the rooms went on and on and that they were all decorated with as much beauty and care as this room. "It's beautiful."

"Don't give me credit for the design," Ronan said. "I hired someone to do it. I don't even know what some of the rooms look like."

She looked at him with surprise. "You don't stay here very often?"

He shifted on his feet. "I've never stayed here. There are a lot of places I own that I've never stayed."

She caught the scent of oranges on the breeze that blew in from the open widow behind her. "Why?"

He shrugged. "When I travel for work, I'm usually in a hurry to get home."

There was no pity in his voice, but she understood then how lonely Ronan's life had been. How he'd run from one job to another, keeping busy so he didn't have to think too long about everything that was missing in his life.

She understood because she recognized it in

herself, the way she'd told herself her life was full when really she was just busy with things that didn't matter because all the things that didn't matter kept her from thinking about the things that did, the things she didn't have.

The stuff she feared she'd never have.

She crossed the room, slid her hands up his chest, and pressed her body to his. "It will do. In fact, I may never leave."

"Promise?" There was humor in the way his mouth twitched, but his eyes shone with the light of truth.

She kissed him, wanting to avoid talk of the future. Here especially, in this city where Elise would be brought for Manifest's party, Julia didn't want to think about anything but getting her sister back alive.

"What now?" she asked. "Want me to boot up the computers and see if there's anything new from home?"

Clay was still working on the invite to the party — what it was, how it could be duplicated — along with trying to get information about the security system inside the villa. He was also crawling the TSA's database for private charters that had filed flight plans into Florence around the date of the next party, hoping to catch unknown Manifest members in the spider's web.

In the meantime, Nick and Declan were spearheading deep background on all of the Whitmore Club members who had traveled to Florence on the dates of previous parties.

Ronan tightened his grip on her. "No work. Not yet. I want to take my woman to dinner in Florence."

She smiled up at him. "Is that what I am? Your woman?"

"Aren't you?" His expression was serious.

She kissed him again and stepped away, afraid of the words that bubbled up in her throat.

Yes. I'm yours. I'll always be yours.

"What does one wear to dinner in Florence?" She kept her tone light. If he'd noticed that she avoided the subject of their relationship, he didn't say anything.

"Whatever one wants," he said. "Better yet wear nothing at all and we'll stay in."

She laughed and headed for the hall they'd passed through when they'd first entered the apartment. "You already offered to take me out. What do you think I am — easy?"

His laugh followed her down the hall.

11

Ronan watched Julia from across the table as she closed her eyes around a bite of chocolate soufflé with salted caramel ice cream. She moaned and he was embarrassed to feel his cock harden in his trousers, the look of bliss on her face all too familiar.

"Oh my god," she moaned. "So good."

She opened her eyes and sat up straighter when she caught him looking at her.

He grinned. "By all means, continue."

She licked her lips, slowly and with feeling, then smirked. "Want a bite?"

He liked the shine in her eyes, the teasing glint. The circumstances surrounding their relationship so far had provided little room for play.

"I'm going to do more than take a bite if you keep it up," he said softly.

Her dark eyes flared amber in the candlelight, her chest rising and falling as her breath quickened. "Promise?"

A surge of lust roared through his body.

"I think it's time for the check."

Up until tonight, he would have said she was most beautiful wearing his T-shirt the morning after sleeping in his arms, her hair tousled around her sleepy face, and while that was definitely still in the running, it was a close call to the way she looked sitting across from him at the Panorama restaurant on the rooftop of La Scalatta hotel, the sky inky and starlit overhead, the city lights shining like a carpet of diamonds below.

After years of keeping it simple, he'd finally availed himself to MIS's international payroll, calling on a woman named Joanne Fuller in Florence, an American expat Declan promised would deliver a selection of appropriate clothing to the apartment well before Ronan's arrival with Julia.

Dec had been right: they'd arrived to find three perfect cocktail dresses hanging in the wardrobe of the apartment's master bedroom. The selection provided enough variety to allow for Julia's preference, but while Ronan would have been happy to see her in any of the dresses, it was hard to imagine any of them being more perfect than the curve-hugging ivory dress she'd chosen, the hemline just far enough above the knee to leave something to the imagination, a matching crocheted shawl draped around her shoulders and providing a glimpse at her bare skin.

She'd pulled her hair back into a loose knot at the back of her neck. Tendrils of her hair had been falling from the front throughout dinner, framing her face in waves.

The waiter brought the bill and Ronan quickly paid, eager to remove the delicate dress from Julia's body, to run his lips and hands over her porcelain skin.

He felt like some kind of magic had taken hold as they walked home over cobblestone streets, the old city keeping her secrets all around them. Boston was far away, his brothers part of another world. Even the specter of Elise seemed to be otherwise occupied for this one night.

Now there was just the two of them, Julia's hand in his, the smell of the Arno layered under the city like a subtle perfume.

She sighed and leaned her head on his arm as they walked, her heels — another item left in the wardrobe by Ms. Fuller — clicking on the old stone streets.

"That was the best meal I've ever had," she said, her voice sleepy.

"I agree." He didn't tell her that it wasn't the food. It wasn't the artichoke and tuna salad, perfectly seasoned, or the tender pistachio-crusted lamb. It wasn't the aged filet with truffle sauce or the perfect wine pairings, each one more sensual on the tongue than the last. It wasn't even the soufflé, although he agreed with Julia that it was magnificent.

It was her, shimmering like the finest jewel amid a city of jewels, the most precious of any artifact in a city overflowing with priceless treasures. Her face had been smoothed of its worry, as if the city had worked its magic on her too.

There had been no talk of Manifest, of the party to which they still had to gain entrance or the men who operated behind Manifest's impenetrable facade. They'd talked instead about their childhood and adolescence, steering clear of the sad stuff as if by unspoken agreement.

Julia had told him about the time she'd cut her own bangs in fifth grade the day before picture day and about the time Elise's date had dumped her the night before prom, prompting Julia to wear a tux and go as her date.

Ronan had told her about the time he'd challenged Nick to climb to the top of the tallest tree at the playground in Peter's Park. Nick fell and broke his arm and their father had blamed Ronan until Nick tried again the same day he got his cast off, proving that, as Thomas Murphy said, "you can only play someone for a fool if they're a fool in the first place."

They'd held hands across the table, their fingers entwined on the fine linen cloth shining with candlelight, and he saw her as she might be if they found Elise and brought her home, if he could take care of things for her so she didn't have to worry so much.

She would bristle if he said it aloud, would insist she was fine, that she had always been fine, that she was used to taking care of things and perfectly capable of doing so.

So he didn't. He just watched her instead, vowing silently to give her everything she deserved.

They crossed one of the bridges stretching across the river, the old-fashioned street lamps casting golden light onto the stone. Julia pulled him to the edge and peered over at the dark waters below before letting her gaze travel to the city, ablaze in lights around the water.

She sighed. "It's so beautiful here."

The naked pleasure on her face made sense of everything. Everything he'd built at MIS, all the money, the property and other investments Nick had pressed on him over the years. The additional zeros that seemed to appear like magic on his financial statements.

Ronan didn't care if he flew Economy class or if he stayed at the Holiday Inn or the Ritz. Up until now the luxuries afforded by MIS had been nothing but a side effect of the business, something else to think about on those occasions when Nick insisted on giving him a financial update or urged him to make a new investment.

But now he saw that there was a reason for all of it. That it could serve the highest purpose of giving Julia everything beautiful the world had to offer.

"I love you." The words escaped his mouth, a violation of the unspoken rule that had crept into their relationship, the rule that said the words were only spoken in the dark, when they were naked and sweaty in each other's arms.

She turned toward him, wrapped her arms around his neck, and pressed her mouth to his. He only had a moment to realize she hadn't said it back before her tongue slipped between his lips. Then he was swept away in the urgency of her exploration, the demand of his own.

The scent of her shampoo, vanilla and sandalwood, hit him with a rush of desire. He swept her mouth slowly and carefully with his tongue, wanting to savor the taste of her, the feel of her yielding to him in the only way she knew how.

When they pulled away, his cock was hard and straining for release.

Julia's eyes shone as she looked up at him, her face flushed. "Take me home."

For a split second he was confused. What did home mean? Boston? The apartment near the river in Florence?

Then he realized it wasn't that complicated.

Wherever she was, that was home. Wherever they were together, that was home.

The thought terrified him. How had she crept into his heart? What if she didn't feel the same way?

He took her hand and started across the bridge, his heart pounding in his chest, not wanting to think too hard about the answers.

12

The apartment was dark when they returned, the lights from the street barely leaking in through the leaves that sheltered the windows from the street below.

She'd realized on the bridge she was a little drunk, had realized it when Ronan told her he loved her, when the words had almost slipped from her own mouth.

It shouldn't matter. She did love him. That was indisputable, and it wasn't like she hadn't told him countless times before.

But after the first time, on the beach after they'd come back from Dubai when the words had slipped like honey from her tongue, she'd taken to saying it in the dark, when she was naked, her limbs entangled with Ronan's, the barrier she'd erected between them lowered.

It was foolish. It didn't change anything. And yet she couldn't help feeling that the darkness offered some form of protection against her own feelings, against the pain she would feel if they later realized their relationship had been a product of Elise's disappearance, like two refugees who turned to each other for comfort in their time of need.

Ronan had said it to her on the bridge as if it were nothing at all.

As if it were everything.

The words had been on the tip of her own tongue. She'd had to kiss him to keep them inside, had demanded he take her home as the emotion welled inside her like a rising tide, to the safety of the bedroom and the sex that made it easier to hide her feelings behind the physical sensation that overtook her body and mind.

Ronan led her through the darkened apartment to the master bedroom. The room was dominated by a massive canopy bed layered in rich blue silks, cast in shadow in the dim light leaking in from the big windows. The other furniture — wardrobes and bureaus and a small settee and coffee table — were smudges at the periphery of the room.

He turned toward her when they reached the bed and cupped her face in his hand. His blue eyes appeared black as he looked down at her.

"This is where I know you're mine."

There was anguish in his voice, and he lowered his mouth to hers, sweeping away her fear in an urgent kiss that sparked a fire at her center.

She wrapped her arms around his neck and gave herself to the electricity flaring outward from her core, sparking along her skin until she was alight with desire for him.

His tongue parried with hers as he trailed a hand down her neck to her shoulder, unbuttoning the shawl that came with the dress, tossing it aside like it was nothing in the face of his need to touch her.

She sighed as he rested his palm at the base of her throat, his fingers spread over her chest above the low neckline of her dress. His hand was a brand against her fevered skin.

She reached for the buttons on his shirt, relieved to look away from the possession she saw burning in his eyes.

Her lips traveling over the muscled perfection of his chest as it was revealed, lingering over each nipple, bending to reach his tight, defined stomach, hard as a washboard.

She shoved the shirt off his shoulders and reached for the button on his trousers.

He grabbed ahold of her hand. "Not yet."

His voice was low and commanding. It was the voice of someone used to being in charge, a voice he only used with her in the bedroom

A voice that made her eager to obey.

He rested his hands on her hips and turned her around, pulling her back against him so hard and fast that she gasped as his erect cock nestled between her ass cheeks.

She leaned back, pressing against the rigid shaft, a vacuum of need opening up between her legs, need that could only be filled by him.

His hands slipped around her waist, moving up over her stomach to cup her breasts, still covered by the dress. She was desperate to remove the barrier between them, to feel his hands on her skin, her nipples between his fingers.

But there was no room for her to move. He had her pressed hard against him, making it clear that he was in charge as the flat of his palms traveled over her stomach, down the front of her thighs.

She moaned as he slid them between her legs, running them slowly up the inside of her thighs, bare under the dress. He made his way inch by inch toward the apex of her desire, her pussy wet and throbbing as his hands came closer, the sparks on her skin turning into a full-fledged wildfire.

He reached the cleft between her legs and slipped his fingers under the nude thong she'd chosen to wear with the dress. She quivered as he brushed her clit and ran his fingers through the petals of her sex.

"You're so fucking wet, Julia." His voice was a murmur in her ear, sending a shiver down her spine, more fuel for the inferno raging in her body.

He slipped his fingers inside her and made slow circles over her clit with his thumb until she was moving with him, her body already reaching for the orgasm it knew he would deliver.

Her dress was bunched up around her hips, her back against his chest as he brought her closer to release, her breath coming in short bursts as she climbed the peak of her orgasm.

She was almost there when he withdrew his hand.

She tried to turn to face him, but he held her in place as he reached for the back of the dress. Her frustration was tempered as he lowered the zipper and pushed the dress off her hips until it fell to the ground, one step closer to being naked in his arms.

The brush of her skin against his bare chest sent another arrow of longing to her pulsing core and she sighed as he lowered his lips to her bare shoulder, leaving a trail of kisses so featherlight she might have thought she imagined them if not for the heat left by his lips.

He cupped her bare breasts from behind as he kissed his way up her neck to her ear, rolling her erect nipples between his thumb and finger as he took her earlobe in his mouth and sucked.

She leaned her head back against his shoulder, her knees weak with need.

He nudged her legs apart with his knee and ripped the scrap of underwear off her body.

He knelt on the floor behind her and she felt his hands around her legs, his hot breath as he buried his face between her thighs.

The absence of his body next to hers made the sensation all the more erotic, nothing but the hot kiss of his mouth against her pussy as he pushed his tongue between her wet folds from behind, the rest of her body devoid of stimulation while inside she burned.

She moaned, her hands coming up to cup her breasts, stimulating her nipples with her fingers as he lapped from the well of her sex, his tongue brushing against her clit just often enough to keep her teetering on the edge of orgasm.

She widened her stance, wanting to give him more access, her release again within reach as his tongue covered every inch of her most sensitive flesh.

She was almost to the top when he withdrew his mouth yet again.

"Fuck you, Ronan," she murmured, out of her mind with lust.

He stood and chuckled in her ear. When he spoke, she caught her own scent on his breath.

"That's the idea."

He nestled one knee between her thighs to keep her legs apart while he bent her over the bed.

She was open for him now, spread out and more ready for him than she'd ever been.

She heard the whisper of his zipper, the crinkle of a condom being opened. Then he was pushing against her opening, his swollen head balanced tantalizingly at her entrance.

She pushed back against him and he gave her ass a slap.

"Patience, lovely."

She whimpered, a shot of exquisite pleasure shooting through every nerve in her body in the moment before he plunged into her with one long, hard thrust.

She cried out, pleasure mingling with the slightest hint of pain coaxing the orgasm to life inside her all over again.

He grabbed onto her hips and dragged out of her inch by inch, letting his tip balance at her entrance before plunging into her again.

"Jesus, Julia," he groaned. "You feel so fucking good. You always feel so fucking good."

She moved with him as he plunged into her again, her body pulling him closer on the downstroke, reluctantly letting him go as he pulled out.

He used his hands to spread her ass cheeks wide, then pushed into her again, impaling her so deeply she felt it in a long shiver up her back.

He moved faster and she knew his own orgasm was close, that he was losing his hold on the control he exerted over her until he couldn't exert it over himself anymore. His thrusts grew more frenzied as he climbed with her, everything between them dissolving as their bodies melted into one, their pleasure and desire mingling as they let go together.

She didn't recognize her own voice as she screamed into the room, her body shuddering with the force of her release.

He groaned as he came, forcing his way through her engorged channel, clamping down on his shaft as her orgasm rocked her body.

She rode the wave as long as she could, giving herself over to the pleasure rocking her body. She didn't want it to end, this moment when they were one without thought, when the ghost of their future was finally obliterated by the power of their desire.

13

Ronan stared down at the boxes on the table in the apartment's living room. He crossed his arms over his chest and shook his head. "No. No way."

"You're going to have to hear us out," Nick said.

Ronan looked at the people in the room, wondering which of these bastards had conspired to put him on the spot with Julia. Nick? Declan? Clay? Monica, the woman who'd arrived with Clay the day before?

His eyes slid to Julia, leaning against the wall by the window. Did she know? Had she somehow convinced Nick and the others to advocate for her?

No. She looked as surprised as he felt.

He returned his attention to the table, picking up the man's Cartier watch. It was heavier than it looked, the links thick and balanced in his hand, the matte gold dial understated with only the slightest shimmer.

"There's a chip in the band," Clay explained. "It has all the data that will be required for you to get into the party."

Ronan turned it over, looking for evidence of the chip. He couldn't see a thing.

He looked at Clay. "This is how it's done?"

This was easier than talking about the other watch, the elaborate women's Van Cleef & Arpels watch with the midnight blue dial that still sat on the table.

The watch clearly meant for Julia.

"This is how it's done," Clay confirmed. "It doesn't have to be a watch, but apparently it's something of a game for the members of Manifest: seeing how subtly they can hide the chip."

"And the chip is the invitation?"

Clay nodded. "It'll be scanned by security on the way in. Yours is coded with Milos Černík's data."

Ronan lifted his eyebrows. "The arms dealer?"

"The same."

"His travel lines up with Manifest's parties in Florence over the past year," Nick explained. "We assume this means he's a member."

"Big assumption," Ronan said.

Nick shrugged. "Not much of a choice."

"What if you're right and Milos shows up to the party?" Ronan asked.

"He's been detained by the Ukrainian government," Declan said. "You can thank Kane for that bit of information."

"Anyone know?" The last thing Ronan needed was to show up using the ID of a guy everyone knew had been pinched.

"They're keeping it on the DL," Dec said. "Hoping to turn him."

"So they scan the watch, Černík's data shows up, and they let me in."

"If all goes well," Nick said.

Ronan didn't bother complaining about the uncertainty. Uncertainty was part and parcel of their business. Nothing was ever certain when you planned to kill a man. You had to roll with the punches.

He set down the Cartier timepiece and picked up the women's watch. It was lovely, with a diamond bezel and white gold band. Tiny diamond chips were sprinkled across the inky blue face, meant to look like stars in a night sky, semiprecious stones set to mimic planets.

"I didn't agree to this." He avoided Julia's eyes, surprised that she'd been quiet so far.

"You need someone else in there with you," Nick said, "and we couldn't find another male identity for me or Dec to appropriate. Julia's chip is coded with the identity of a Czech heiress who's attended the parties with Černík in the past. Rumor has it she has interesting... appetites of her own."

Ronan turned over the watch and looked at the band. The chip was as invisible on the women's watch as it had been on the Cartier watch meant for him.

He set it down and closed the lid on its box, liking the finality of the sound. "I'll go alone."

"That would be stupid," Declan said.

Ronan was surprised to see his brother's blue eyes flash with anger. Declan rarely got angry about anything. What was there to be angry about when life was one big party and you were always the guest of honor?

"I've done plenty of jobs alone," Ronan said. "In fact, you may remember that until recently that's how I worked most of the time."

"This isn't like the other times," Nick said. His arms were crossed over his chest, mimicking Ronan's posture when he'd first laid eyes on the watch meant for Julia. "Security is heavy, and you're not going in for a quiet kill and a quick exit. If Elise is there, you may need help creating a distraction to get to her. If you find her, you may need help convincing her to go with you."

"I can handle myself," Julia said quietly.

He turned toward her, still leaning against the wall. There was no triumph in her gaze, only the same resignation that had begun leaking through his veins while Nick and Declan made their case.

"She knows how to use a weapon." Ronan cursed the day he'd told Nick that Julia had been packing when they went to Dubai, cursed the day Julia had told Nick and Declan over beers that her grandfather had taught her and Elise to shoot when they were teenagers. "She might not be an expert, but you could do worse for backup."

"It's not about that." Ronan knew how Julia prided herself on being an asset instead of a burden.

He could hardly look at her when she came to stand next to him. Doing so made him want to lock her away, keep her from anything that might hurt her, even if it meant she hated him for it.

He knew it wasn't an option even as the thought crossed his mind. She might forgive him for doing it, but she would never forgive him for leaving Elise behind again, and Nick and Declan were right: the rescue mission was a two-person job.

"I know I'm not as experienced as Nick or Dec," she said. "I'll take orders from you, I promise."

It was a statement, not a plea, and he knew he'd lost.

14

Julia stood in front of the full-length mirror and studied her reflection. The dress was beautiful, a brilliant shade of purple silk structured into a column and suspended from one shoulder, but it wasn't right.

She met the eyes of the dark-haired woman in the mirror and tried to find a way to say as much without offending her.

"Not quite right, is it?" Joanne Fuller asked.

Julia shook her head. "I'm sorry. I'm being difficult."

Joanne made a sound of dismissal. "Don't be ridiculous, darling. An evening gown should feel like a new lover. If you're not enamored, it's not right, and it must be right. Off you go then."

Julia unzipped the gown, relieved Joanne understood, although Julia wouldn't have thought to put it so eloquently.

Then again, everything about Joanne Fuller was eloquent. An American living in Florence so long her English had developed a slight accent, Joanne had in every way become a fashionable Italian signora, from her luscious dark hair to her always precise red lipstick to the tailored clothing that hugged her hourglass figure in all the right places.

According to Ronan, Joanne was kept on retainer for those occasions when Nick or Declan needed a woman's touch in Italy. Julia had been jealous until Ronan confided he'd never before availed himself of Joanne's services.

She handed the purple gown to Joanne and stood in her underwear, waiting as Joanne surveyed the rack of clothing that had been wheeled into the apartment by two uniformed men at the start of the afternoon.

She'd been shy at first — she wasn't used to standing around half-undressed with anyone but her sister — but she'd had no choice but to set modesty aside as Joanne presented her with gown after gown, prodding Julia's flesh as she arranged Julia's body in each selection.

She was trying not to think too hard about the

reason for the gown, the fact that in four days she and Ronan would have to lie their way into Manifest's monthly party, Ronan as Milos Černík and Julia under the guise of the heiress named Anuska Král.

They had no idea what kind of verification process would be required to enter the party, whether the chips Clay had coded with their identifying data would be enough or whether they'd have to submit to a visual verification or questions about their past. To be safe, Julia had cultivated a Czech accent, dyed her hair a lighter shade of blond, and she planned to wear blue contacts the night of the party to better match Anuska's appearance. She'd also studied Anuska's background, memorizing her parents' names and the names of the schools she'd attended as a child.

Ronan had done the same with the details of Milos Černík's identity, although he had a leg up on Julia, both because he already knew something about Černík and because their basic stats — height, weight, hair color — were close enough to be considered the same.

"Ah, I think I have it." Joanne held out a voluminous gown in crushed indigo velvet, embroidered flowers adorning the skirt and bodice in a riot of color. "It's ready-to-wear, but quite fabulous."

"I don't know..." Julia usually preferred simple lines and monochromatic colors. This looked like an ad she'd once seen for Dolce and Gabbana featuring sensuous Italian women with heavily made-up faces sitting at an outdoor cafe.

Joanne met her eyes. "Will you trust me?"

Julia took the dress with a nod and turned toward the mirror.

It slipped over her head like a breeze, settling as softly as a cloud on her body. Joanne stepped behind her to work the zipper and Julia saw that while the skirt was soft and full, the bodice, held up by the thinnest of straps, was actually quite fitted, the intricate flowers on the bodice making her torso look almost like a butterfly.

It was exquisite.

Joanne pulled back Julia's hair. "I think there's just enough blue in the flowers to bring out the color in the contacts you'll be wearing." Julia registered surprise that Joanne knew about the contacts. She wondered how much the older woman knew about MIS's business. "And this is very Italian, dear. You'll stand out because you're stunning, of course, but you'll also look like you belong, and I think that will be important."

The dress fit her like a dream, like the dream of a woman she might have been, a woman she might still be if that's what she wanted.

Julia met Joanne's eyes in the mirror. "I think you're right."

Joanne smiled. "Lovely. Now let's see what we have in the way of shoes."

Julia's eyes remained on the mirror as Joanne turned to a series of boxes lining the floor. She wondered if Ronan would like the dress, then chided herself for being ridiculous.

They hadn't discussed the fact that she was going to the party with him, not privately, but she knew he was livid about it. She'd heard him fighting with Nick and Declan after she'd gone to bed, arguing that they should have come to him first before mentioning it in front of her.

"You would have found a way to argue the point," Nick had said.

"Damn right," Ronan had growled.

Julia had had to resist the urge to break up the argument, to remind Ronan that she was a grown woman who didn't want or need to be sheltered from the details of her sister's rescue. The fight was between Ronan and his brothers. It wasn't her business.

She was going, which was all she cared about. She wasn't going to risk letting Elise slip through her fingers again, and she wanted to be the first person her sister saw when she knew someone had finally come for her.

"Let's try these," Joanne said, holding out a pair of strappy black heels somewhere between Fashion Week and Stevie Nicks circa 1977.

Julia bent to put them on her feet, then stood to look at her reflection. There was something of Elise staring back at her in the elegant dress, the lighter hair catching the late afternoon sun slanting through the apartment's big windows.

She thought again of Ronan, of the weighty silences that had been between them in the days since he'd accepted she would attend the Manifest party at his side. She knew he wasn't angry at her — at the situation maybe, at Nick and Declan, but not at her.

Still, the tension between them, diffused only when she was naked in his arms, scared her. She couldn't help wondering if this was the beginning of the end, one more thing in a line of things that would slowly undo them until Elise was finally brought home and they had no reason to be together at all.

15

Ronan sat in the back of the limo and watched the outskirts of Florence pass by on the other side of the window. He was hyperaware of Julia next to him, the scent of her perfume taunting him like a dream to which he was too eager to return.

She looked magnificent, although to his mind no more magnificent than she looked in jeans and bare feet, or in the oversized boxer shorts she sometimes wore around the house when she wore no makeup and left her hair loose and messy around her face or pulled up into a haphazard knot at the top of her head.

Still, the dress highlighted the perfection of her breasts, the toned length of her arms, and the slender line of her neck. Her hair was twisted not into a casual knot, but slicked back into an almost severe twist, and her features looked more pronounced thanks to the makeup artist Joanne Fuller had sent over to help Julia prepare for the party.

She looked like a slightly different version of herself, and when he'd searched her eyes for the amber fire that sometimes sparked there, he'd found only a clear and unsettling shade of blue.

She was still his Julia, he knew that, knew it from the way she came to life in his arms at night, the way she allowed him to occupy her body even if a dark corner of her soul was still off-limits, but he was eager to be done with this night. Eager to bring Elise home and prove to Julia that his love for her would be unchanged, to cook for her and take Chief for walks on the beach and sleep late on Sundays.

He would do it as long as it took to earn her trust. He would do it forever.

She reached for his hand and he looked over at her across the darkness in the backseat of the limo, driven by Nick, who would be forced to leave Ronan and Julia at the gate of the villa in the city's Firenze district in keeping with Manifest protocol.

No one was allowed on the grounds without a

chip, something Braden Kane had passed along from his contact on the FVEY task force.

"It will be okay," she said.

"I know." It was something he didn't doubt. He knew it would be okay because someone would hurt Julia over his dead body, and he had a habit of not turning up dead even when the odds were against him.

The minute he'd accepted that Julia would be attending the party, getting her out alive had become his prime objective. It wasn't something he could tell her. She had to think he would risk everything to save Elise, but there was no way in hell he would let anything happen to Julia. If that meant hauling her out of the place the way he had in Dubai, so be it.

If it meant she hated him, so be it.

He turned his thoughts to the villa that was host to the party. Even with Braden Kane's sources, they'd been able to gain precious little information about the security they could expect inside.

It wasn't unheard of. Ronan had been in more than one situation with too little information. But he hadn't had Julia with him in those situations. Now the lack of information felt like the weakness it was, the potential consequences all too real.

He could assume there would be heavy security at the gate where their chips would be scanned for the first time and again at the front door to the villa. After that, it was anybody's guess.

The one thing they did have was a decent grasp on the layout of the villa. A search through the digital building archives for the city had given Clay the basics, which included six exits, eight balconies, and a series of tunnels that had once been used in the operation of an onsite vineyard.

The tunnels were a last resort. They hadn't been used in over a hundred years, but with all the doors and balconies, Ronan was fairly certain they wouldn't have to make an exit underground.

They'd gone over the layout more times than Ronan could count, he and Julia agreeing on three meeting places in the event that they got separated. They would try first for the sunroom at the back of the house. If anything prevented them from meeting there, they would head for the kitchen, which also happened to have a set of doors leading to the back terrace.

If the first two options failed, they would meet at the entrance to the tunnels.

He'd quizzed Julia incessantly on the details of

her identity as Anuska Král. She'd passed with flying colors, delivering each lie so convincingly he'd begun to wonder where she'd honed the ability.

The limo slowed down as they approached a line of brake lights, other limos stopped as they made their way to the gate of the villa.

The privacy window rolled down with an electric hum.

"You ready for this?" Nick asked from the driver's seat.

"Ready," Julia said.

Ronan wished there was more fear in her voice, that there was some evidence that she understood the danger of the situation in which they would soon find themselves. There was too much they didn't know, too much that could go wrong, and they weren't even sure Elise would be among the girls being brought to Manifest's showcase.

He had the urge to tell Nick to turn around, to take Julia straight to the airport and force her onto the plane back to Boston, to throw up his hands and tell John Taylor it had been a mistake to take the job, that they couldn't help him.

But it was too late for that. For one thing, he couldn't turn his back on Elise Berenger, couldn't turn his back on the other girls like her now that he had a chance of saving even some of them.

For another, he could no longer deny that he was deeply and hopelessly in love with Julia — and there would be no future with Julia without the safe return of her sister.

16

Julia squeezed Ronan's hand as the limo's back door was opened by one of the guards standing outside the gate to the villa. She forced a bored expression onto her face — she'd studied the few pictures of Anuska Král she could find online and found that this was her most often utilized expression — and stepped from the limo with as much dismissive entitlement as she could muster.

"Identification," the guard said in accented English. He held a tablet in one hand, a tiny digital wand in the other.

She was aware of Ronan stepping from the limo behind her as she offered the guard her wrist, the diamond watch band glittering in the lights from the cars still in line.

She looked around, trying to look vaguely impatient while he brought the wand up against the watch. Her heart hammered in her chest, the gun she'd strapped under the skirt of her dress burning against her thigh.

A beep sounded from the tablet and the guard looked from its display to Julia's face, then back again.

He stepped back and waved her through. She was momentarily relieved she hadn't had to answer any questions, then remembered that she wasn't done yet: there would be a check at the front door of the villa, assuming they made it that far.

She stepped through the iron gate and waited on a cobblestone path while Ronan proffered his own wrist. Not wanting to seem concerned, she glanced around, watching as another guest — a woman with striking dark hair and eyes so light gray they appeared almost silver — offered the back of her neck to one of the guard's wands.

Did she have the chip embedded in her skin?

Julia tried to get a better look without being too obvious and thought she caught sight of a tattoo that might have been the Manifest symbol at the woman's hairline. A moment later the guard cross-checked a picture on his tablet against the face of the woman in front of him.

She returned her gaze to Ronan as the first guard waved him through.

He held out his arm, and Julia tried to hide the trembling of her hand as she took it. It was only the first test, but they'd passed, which meant they were one step closer to Elise.

The air was soft and fragrant, the walkway leading to the villa lined with trees strung with white lights. It might have been a black-tie party for celebrities or wealthy philanthropists, and Julia's stomach turned as she thought about everything they'd learned about Manifest: trafficking, arms dealing to terrorist groups, even black market organ harvesting.

She had to get Elise away from these people, and it had to be tonight. If Braden Kane was right — and Ronan said his sources were as good as they got — the girls would soon be auctioned.

After that, finding them would be next to impossible.

She reconsidered their decision not to use a comms system to allow for communication between Nick, Declan, Clay, and her and Ronan. Deep down she knew it had been the right choice — they couldn't risk being caught with it, especially since so much of the security inside the villa was unknown

— but she still hated the fact that she and Ronan were on their own.

It felt way too much like walking into a lion's den.

"Easy," Ronan said next to her.

She hadn't realized that she'd tightened her grip on his arm. "I'm okay."

"Good. Stay close," he said as they approached the front door to the villa.

They took their place in line behind a handful of other people waiting to enter the villa. She let her gaze skim over the faces around her, not wanting to give anyone reason to make eye contact.

She wasn't under any illusions: she didn't look enough like Anuska Král to fool anyone who knew the woman well. But the people around her didn't know she was posing as the Czech heiress. Only the guards armed with tablets would know that, and presumably they weren't well acquainted with any of the guests. They would do exactly what the guard at the gate did — look at her picture on the tablet and compare it to Julia standing in front of them.

She looked enough like Anuska Král to pass under those circumstances, something she'd proven at the gate. Her best bet with everyone else was to avoid in-depth conversation, keep a low profile.

There was only one person in front of them in

the line for the door, a diminutive man in a tux that looked vaguely familiar to Julia, his bald head shining under the lights at the front of the house.

The guard at the door held a wand to the man's cufflink, looked at the tablet, and waved him in without question.

Would it be that simple? Another easy pass into the house?

She didn't dare hope as she stepped up to the guard.

He held out a satin bag and she dropped in the burner phone Ronan had given her. Braden had tipped them off about the phone check, and they'd both brought untraceable phones that could be left behind.

The guard lifted the wand and she held out her hand, looking around like it was all a formality she shouldn't have to bear.

"Name?"

"Pardon me?" She was careful to use the accent she'd been practicing.

The guard looked into her eyes. "Your name."

She tried to look mildly offended. "Anuska Král."

"Identification number."

Why was she being asked questions when the

man in front of her had been allowed to pass without so much as a word?

She lifted her chin and rattled off Anuska Král's passport number. It was another tidbit from the man named Kane: passport numbers were used as Manifest ID numbers.

The man checked the number against the tablet and looked again at Julia's face, his eyes moving over her features.

She met his gaze, trying to convey the superiority of wealth and privilege that must go hand in hand with inheriting so much money that you had nothing better to do than attend parties with corrupt rich people who sought pleasure from imprisoned women who couldn't fight back.

It seemed like an eternity before he blinked.

He tipped his head toward the house and Julia stepped in, standing aside while she waited for Ronan to pass the same inspection. Instead the guard scanned Ronan's watch, glanced at the tablet, and waved him forward without another word.

They were in.

17

Every nerve in Ronan's body was on high alert as they made their way through the crowd into the house. Had he been alone, it would have been just another job, if slightly more challenging given that he had to get someone else out alive.

With Julia by his side it felt too much like chumming shark infested waters with fresh meat.

The house was homier than he'd expected. It might have been the country estate of a wealthy Italian family, filled with luxurious but comfortable furniture and French doors open to the terraces that surrounded the house.

The ceiling soared to worn wood timber overhead and the walls were warm textured plaster. It was a house he would have enjoyed spending time in under other circumstances.

They made their way farther inside and he noted the suited guards positioned throughout the rooms of the first floor. He knew they were packing from the bulges under their jackets — he would have expected no less — and he was unsurprised to find two of them stationed at the bottom of the front staircase.

If the house were set up like the Whitmore Club, they would bring the girls to the second and third floors. He could only assume they hadn't yet arrived: no one approached the stairs, and the crowd seemed content to drink and mingle.

A uniformed server stopped at their side with a tray of champagne. Ronan took a glass and handed it to Julia, then took one for himself.

She touched her glass to his in a wordless toast and he knew she was thinking about Elise, hoping this would be the day they would finally bring her sister home.

He turned his attention to the crowd around them. He recognized a handful of business titans, plus a couple of trust fund babies from the news. The other faces blended into a sea of polished flesh, tuxedos, silk and satin gowns.

It was the women who bothered him most. It

shouldn't have mattered, but what kind of woman did you have to be to look the other way while men traded in members of your own gender, members who had spent centuries being used and abused by men, fighting and dying for the chance to be free?

Was it possible some of them didn't know that the party was a Manifest showcase for the "assets" of an upcoming sale?

It was hard to imagine. The women had to know. Maybe it was just a relief to find themselves on the other side of the transaction for once. From that perspective, they seemed slightly less guilty than the men who'd always been on the other side.

That was where he needed to focus his anger.

"How long?"

He looked at Julia, impressed that she'd remembered to use the Czech accent she'd practiced when they'd been running Anuska Král's background. It wasn't perfect, but it was close enough for anyone who might overhear or for anyone trying to make small talk with her.

"Soon," he said.

They'd argued about which of them would create the distraction that would get the other one upstairs until he realized he wouldn't be happy with any of the potential solutions unless they involved Julia not being at the party at all. Finally he'd had to agree that it was best for him to create the distraction.

The less attention paid to Julia at a party like this one the better.

She would use the time to slip upstairs via one of the three back staircases. Once there she would search the rooms for Elise, freeing anyone else she might come upon at the same time.

Ronan would keep everyone occupied downstairs for ten minutes, after which he would meet Julia — and hopefully Elise — at one of the predetermined meeting points.

It wasn't as clear-cut as he would have liked. In fact, it was a lot like the way he worked when he was alone, when he had to remain flexible, roll with the punches of whatever awaited him: fine under those circumstances but not ideal when he was worried about getting Julia out alive.

There was no way around it. There were too many wild cards at the party, too much they didn't know. It would take weeks to case the Florence parties adequately enough to come up with a solid plan that took into account the number of guards, the weapons they carried, security cameras, and all the other factors that went into developing a foolproof exit plan.

Elise didn't have weeks.

"Don't forget to mark the time," Ronan said quietly. "Ten minutes. That's it, whether you find her or not."

It was his biggest fear: that Julia wouldn't stop looking once she started, that she would search under every bed and in every closet once she was upstairs, even if the clock ran out. It would force him to go up after her, endangering them both, making it less likely that he would be able to get her out alive.

She'd promised to take her cues from him, to follow his orders once they were inside, but he knew all too well how the desire to save someone you loved could make you do stupid things, rash things.

He'd done those things in Erin's name. He was doing them now for Julia.

Julia gave him an almost imperceptible nod. It was as close as he would get to an assurance.

The number of guests making their way into the house from the foyer had slowed to a trickle. The party was well under way, the murmur of conversation a hum that vied for attention with the music — an unexpected mix of EDM and techno-punk —

that was being piped into the rooms through invisible speakers.

It was time.

He sat his empty glass on a passing tray and spoke without looking at Julia. "See you soon."

18

Julia watched Ronan work his way through the crowd, purposefully jostling the other guests as he went. There was a hint of enjoyment in the way he shoved, sloshing flutes of champagne held in manicured fingers, displacing people who weren't used to being displaced.

She couldn't say that she blamed him.

She hated being here, knowing these people were using women like Elise, knowing the ones who weren't were looking the other way.

She looked at the faces around her and had to resist the urge to scream. They were polished and coiffed, wearing the latest designer fashion and swilling expensive champagne like water, but it was all a lie, a pretty veneer to cover up a corrupt and poisonous ideology that made them believe the rules didn't apply to them.

No wonder Ronan had shunned outward displays of his wealth. He'd seen the underside of high society more than most.

She trailed far enough behind him that it wouldn't look like she was following, waiting to stop until she reached the arched doorway of the large room where they'd been standing. From this vantage point she could see the foyer — as big as her whole apartment in Boston — where Ronan had shoved into one of the guards.

The guard said something Julia couldn't hear, his expression a warning to Ronan, who had adopted a look of belligerent aggression.

A ripple moved through the people in the foyer, two men and a couple who'd just arrived moving toward the room where Julia stood. They looked from Ronan to the guard, then continued into the house. Julia caught the scent of expensive cologne as one of the men passed within feet of her, Ronan's disturbance already behind him.

These were people used to having messes and unpleasant circumstances cleaned up by others. It probably wasn't the first time someone had gotten confrontational at a Manifest party: their members were rich but they were still human.

Julia removed a compact from her clutch and pretended to check her face as Ronan shoved against a second guard. The first guard spoke into the mouthpiece of a headset tucked into his ear. Less than a minute later, two more guards appeared from the back of the house and moved in around Ronan, muttering something unintelligible to Julia's ears.

Ronan caught her eye just before his arm shot out, his fist landing in the middle of the first guard's face.

The man stumbled backwards, knocking into a marble console table near the entrance. A large Satsuma vase toppled, falling to the floor with a crash.

The two guards by the stairs moved toward the melee in the foyer.

The plan was clear: get to the second and third floors while Ronan created a distraction.

It had sounded simple, but that had been before Ronan was surrounded by men with guns. She had to fight the impulse to go to him, to start fighting off the guards closing around him.

He was a grown man. This was his work. He knew what he was doing.

She glanced at her watch and forced herself to move past the stairs, her head at an imperious tilt, as if she had every right to explore the villa at her leisure.

The rooms on the blueprint accessed by Clay had been unlabeled, which made sense given their age, and she kept the house's floor plan in her mind's eye as she moved past the large rooms, marking them off as she headed for one of three rooms that had a staircase.

She didn't know if her breach of the Whitmore Club had led to additional security at other Manifest properties, but she would save the kitchen stairs as a last resort in case they expected her to use the same method twice.

She came to a room with a set of closed wooden doors. If she was right, this should be the first of the rooms with a staircase leading to the upper floors.

She pushed through the doors without hesitation. Entitlement was the key to access. If she acted like she had every right to be there, she was less likely to be stopped and questioned.

The room was dimly lit with green table lamps, every wall lined with shelves groaning with books. She'd barely stepped into the room when she noticed two men kissing on a tufted leather sofa.

One of them looked up, his eyes glassy, his gaze sweeping Julia's body. "Care to join us, darling?"

"I'm sorry. Excuse me." She bowed out of the room, closing the doors behind her.

Damn...

She crossed the hall and headed toward the other room that should have a staircase. Its doors were closed as well, and she took a deep breath before opening it, bracing herself for another unexpected surprise.

The room was empty, a massive desk dominating one end of the room, two loveseats facing each other over an antique coffee table and rug.

She stepped inside and closed the door behind her, then checked her watch. Three minutes had passed since Ronan had initiated the distraction. She was only guaranteed seven more minutes to get upstairs. Once there, it was anybody's guess how much time she had.

She made her way deeper into the darkened room, searching its periphery for the staircase that had appeared on the blueprints. When she came to a door set into a wood panel in one of the corners, she knew she'd found it.

She tried the knob and was unsurprised to find it locked. It took her less than ten seconds to remove the pick set she'd tucked into her clutch after hours practicing with it in the days leading up to the party.

Like so much about the event, they'd had no idea if the secondary staircases would be hidden behind doors and whether those doors would be locked. Working the lock picks on the doors in Ronan's Florence apartment had been maddening, but now she was glad Ronan had insisted she learn. She wasn't an expert, but she'd gotten fairly quick with basic locks.

She bent down to take a look at the mechanism. It was old, larger than a modern lock. She chose a pick that looked to be the right size, but it proved to be slightly too big, so she sized down one pick. This one fit easily into the lock.

She forced herself to breathe slow and easy as she felt for the tumblers inside the lock, waiting for the pick to clear them one by one. The first time, she turned the pick too fast, before the final tumbler had cleared.

She took a breath and tried again, backing the pick out of the lock and turning slowly.

The lock clicked and the door swung open.

She stepped into a wood-paneled stairwell and started up a flight of stairs. The stairwell was similar to the one at the Whitmore Club, but this one was older, the stone walls concealing a chilly vestibule that smelled of age and damp.

She reached the door on the second floor landing and was relieved to find it unlocked. She couldn't see the face of her watch in the stairwell, but she knew she was running out of time.

She opened the door and stepped onto a carpeted hallway.

The hall was lined with doors, some open and some closed, sconces casting shadows against the textured plaster of the villa's old walls. Oil portraits marched down the walls, a series of severe but sensuous looking men and women with dark hair and brooding eyes watching as she made her way to the first door, open a couple of inches.

She'd barely stepped into the room when she heard voices at the other end of the hall.

She left the door open an inch and listened as two men came closer, the conversation getting louder as they neared the room in which she hid.

"... possible security breach. Orders are to put the charter on hold. The choppers too," one man said.

"They're ready to land." The second man spoke in English accented with Italian. Or was it French?

"I don't give the orders," the first man said.

The second man cursed in Italian. "He's a drunk. Why don't they clear him out and be done with it?"

"You know how they've been lately. Protocols were ramped up after the breach in Dubai. They're being careful."

... put the charter on hold. The choppers too.
They're ready to land...

Julia balled her fists at her side, resisting the urge to plunge them into the wall against her back. Had Ronan's distraction served the purpose of preventing Elise and the other women from being brought to the party?

She looked around the room, taking in the desk against the window and thinking about the other doors lining the second floor hallway.

She looked at her watch, forcing herself to focus. She couldn't afford to be emotional. Not when Elise was out there, still counting on Julia to find her.

It had been eight minutes since Ronan started picking a fight with the guards. Technically she only had two minutes before they were supposed to meet, but there was no way she was going to call the mission a loss because Elise wasn't in the building.

The guards had moved toward the stairs, their voices evaporating as they stepped into the stairwell.

She turned the knob, closing the door with a quiet click, and moved deeper into the room.

She would move as quickly as she could. Ronan would find a way to wait for her.

She knew he would.

19

Ronan couldn't look at his watch but an instinctual clock in his head ticked down the time as he punched and kicked the guards, taking a few hits along the way to draw out the fight.

He was surprised they hadn't pulled a weapon on him yet. He could only assume they were hesitant to take the fight to the extreme in front of the guests.

He'd been gratified to see additional guards entering the large foyer, lining the periphery of the area, waiting to be called into action. With any luck they'd left other parts of the house unguarded, making it easier for Julia to get to Elise.

He figured he had roughly two minutes before Julia would be at one of their predetermined meeting spots.

He looked at the two guards circling him. Blood dripped from the nose of the tall, skinny one. The meaty one was breathing hard.

He could kill two minutes no problem.

20

She found what she was looking for in the third room she tried. By then she wasn't surprised. In spite of its untraceable ownership, the villa obviously wasn't some generic meeting place for Manifest.

Someone lived here — or stayed here at least some of the time.

The realization had only teased the back of her mind when she'd been on the first floor — the desk in the room she'd used to access the staircase a giveaway that the room might be someone's work space.

But when she'd gotten to the second floor, it had become obvious. There was another desk in the first room, and while there hadn't been any photographs or overtly personal artifacts, there had been evidence that the desk was used on a regular basis

— pens, paper clips, a half-empty pack of breath mints, two cigars, a gold lighter.

She hadn't found anything of note in the desk, but the possibility that the villa was used for more than parties gave her hope and she'd moved through the next room as quickly as possible, all too aware of the ticking clock, the fact that Ronan would be heading to one of their meeting places.

She'd just opened the top drawer of a sideboard that seemed to act as a bar in the third room when an alarm pealed though the house.

It took her a few seconds to realize that's what the sound — a low, rhythmic squeal — was. It could only mean one thing: Ronan was on the loose downstairs, which meant the place would be on lockdown as they tried to find him, and quite possibly as they tried to find her, since she'd arrived on his arm and was now conspicuously absent.

For a split second, she hesitated. Her time was up. Elise wasn't here, wasn't going to be here. Ronan wouldn't leave without her, and every second he waited meant more exposure, a greater possibility of being caught.

She knew better than to think the people behind Manifest would simply call the police if they caught Ronan, but if she left now, it was all for nothing: the weeks of planning, of biding their time in Florence, the exposure they'd subjected themselves to by attending the party.

She turned back to the sideboard. The top drawer was empty, but when she opened the second one her breath caught in her throat: a series of manila folders were lined up against the green felt interior.

She grabbed for the first folder as the alarm echoed through the house, praying it was something, anything, that would take them closer to Elise.

Her eyes skimmed the page. It looked like a delivery receipt for a container ship in the port of Naples, an illegible signature scrawled on the receipt line. Her fingers itched for her phone and a way to take a photograph of the signature to decipher later.

She flipped through the page inside the folder, hoping for a manifest, something that would tell her what had been brought into port for the people behind Manifest, but there was only a series of receipts like the first one — dates and a signature acknowledging receipt of the shipping container.

She filed away the dates, all of them the month before, in April, and set the folder aside, scrambling for the one behind it.

When she opened it, she was met with the image

of a young woman with dark hair and haunted eyes, her cheeks hollow, a purple bruise shadowing her right eye.

Julia's stomach rolled over when she saw the title of the page: Asset #US4879KM.

What kind of audacity did Manifest have to have to keep a hard copy of their ongoing crimes? She chided herself for her naivety. The world was full of criminals who'd been getting away with their crimes for so long they assumed they were invincible.

She flipped through the pages behind the first one and was met with more pictures of more women, some of them wearing looks of defeat while others lifted their chins at the person behind the camera as if in challenge, all of them with the same haunted look of the first woman.

A look that said they'd seen too much, had endured too much.

She was three-quarters of the way through the images when she was met with her sister's familiar gaze.

Elise stared back with a mixture of resignation and defiance Julia knew well. Her face was unmarked, but two faint red lines marked the portion of her neck that was visible in the picture.

Julia combed the page carefully, her eyes snagging on a date at the bottom.

DOS: 2019/June/25

LOC: 36.8915° N, 27.2877° E

The second line was a coordinate, but she had no idea what the first line referred to.

Distant shouting sounded from somewhere in the house, but she couldn't tell if it was down the hall, in one of the stairwells, or somewhere else.

She thought about taking the folder with her, then decided it would be stupid. Better to let Manifest — and whoever lived or worked in this house — think their secrets hadn't been uncovered.

She memorized the coordinates and the date on Elise's page and reluctantly put it back where she found it along with the other folders.

Then she ran for the door.

21

It wasn't the first time Ronan was glad he'd brought the taser. They hadn't been patted down for weapons on arrival at the party — a professional courtesy for Manifest guests — but everyone expected a gun.

A taser was rarely considered, and its use was inevitably followed by a dramatic pause during which everyone involved stopped to think, *"Did he just use a fucking taser?"*

Aside from the obvious advantage of giving him a few seconds head start in the ensuing chase, he had to admit that he enjoyed the shock value.

The taser only worked once before it had to be charged, but it was enough. He ducked out of the circle of guards and slipped through the crowd of onlookers, whose shock added to his sense of satisfaction. He could only assume it had been awhile — or maybe never — since one of their sick little parties had been disrupted.

By the time the guards were in full-fledged chase, the alarm ringing through the house with an eerie squawk, he'd made it to the kitchen.

He hoped Julia skipped trying the first two meeting places. They hadn't known about the alarm, hadn't anticipated the added attention. There was no way one of their first two meeting places would be accessible now.

He barreled through the cooks and servers, knocking over trays of champagne and hors d'oeuvres on his way to the door at the back of the kitchen that led to the tunnels under the villa.

There was no way to know if it was still accessible — the blueprints had been a hundred years old — but Ronan was betting on the fact that modern renovations of historical properties rarely allowed for the demolition of historical details.

The doorframe was small, short enough that he made a mental note to duck when he opened the door. When he did, he saw that he'd been right: a narrow stairway descended into the darkness below, cobwebs hanging from the old stone ceiling.

He shut the door behind him, wondering if the

kitchen staff would think to tell anyone about him, wondering if anyone would think to ask.

The stairs were stone and almost seemed to be carved into the building's foundation. They went on forever, turning and twisting as they took him farther underground until he felt like he'd entered an alternate dimension, one where he would step from the tunnels and find that his whole life had passed him by.

He was almost surprised when he finally hit the ground, his foot reaching into the darkness for a step that wasn't there.

He took a couple steps forward and was able to make out the beginnings of the old tunnel, crumbling brick arching overhead.

There was no sign of Julia.

He called her name to be sure she wasn't hiding in the shadows, then cursed when she didn't answer. There hadn't been time to look at his watch when he'd been running from the guards, and it was too dark to see it in the tunnel, but he knew instinctively that they were already past the ten-minute time limit they'd set for Julia to find Elise.

Fear simmered inside him, but he forced himself to ignore it, to turn to the cold reason that always got him out of a tight spot.

Only two things could have caused her delay: she'd either found something — hopefully Elise — and it was taking longer than they'd expected for her to make her way to their meeting point, or she'd been caught.

There was no way to know which unless he returned to the house, and returning to the house meant he wouldn't be there if Julia showed, not to mention a greater chance of getting caught.

He'd escaped once. Twice was too lucky, even for him.

He would wait. Julia was smart and resourceful. She would show, and if she didn't he would burn the place down looking for her.

He'd barely come to the decision when he heard feet on the steps above him.

Had the kitchen staff alerted security to the fact that a man had torn through the kitchen on his way to a door most of them had probably never noticed? Was security doing their due diligence, checking every possible escape route?

He stepped into the shadows and put his back against the tunnel's cold wall as he waited, the footsteps getting louder as the person approached the bottom of the staircase.

It seemed to take forever, the tunnel swallowing

time in the same way it had on his way down the stairs. There was a pause when the person finally reached the bottom.

"Ronan?" Julia's voice was soft and tentative.

"Jesus christ." He stepped from the shadows and pulled her into his arms, then took her face in his hand, inspecting it for signs of harm. "Are you all right?"

"I'm fine," she said. "They're not bringing the girls. I think the fight with the guards set off some kind of alarm, some kind of protocol, but — "

"They weren't there?" He'd risked Julia's life and Elise hadn't even gotten to the building.

"No, but I'm trying to tell you I found something," she said in a rush. "Some kind of... asset list..." She shook her head. "I don't want to call it that but that's what it said."

He glanced back at the stairs, half expecting to hear feet descending the staircase. "Slow down. I'm not getting what you're saying."

"There was a folder with pictures of women," she said, her eyes wide in the dark. "Elise was there too, and there was a date in June and... coordinates or something."

Coordinates. Another meeting place for the

girls? The location of the auction that was supposed to take place after tonight's showcase?

"Okay," he said, "that's good. It's something. But we have to go."

She glanced behind her. "Elise..."

"You said she wasn't there," he said gently.

"I know." Her voice sounded so forlorn that he pulled her back into his arms. "We're not done," he said into her hair. "We'll find her, I promise. But right now, we have to get out of here."

He wasn't even sure the tunnel would give them an unobstructed exit — there was no way to know for sure based on the old blueprints — but it was the only shot they had, and the sooner they started walking, the sooner they'd find out.

"What if we never get another chance?" she asked, her voice small.

"Do you trust me?" he asked.

She nodded.

"We'll get another chance." He took her hand. "Let's go."

They stepped into the darkness.

22

Julia rose through the water, her breathing regular and even, Ronan's face, covered by his face mask, a few inches from hers.

After two weeks of diving, she was finally used to the muffled silence of being underwater, the rhythmic sound of her breath working its way through the hoses attached to the oxygen tank on her back. After her initial panic, she'd even come to look forward to it thanks to the hours she'd spent underwater since they'd arrived in Greece.

She emerged at the surface a moment before Ronan and looked up to see Nick peering over the edge of the boat.

"Good job," he said. "That was a half hour."

She removed her face mask — a specialty mask that allowed them to communicated with each other under water — and grinned. During her first dive, she'd been overcome with claustrophobia, convinced she couldn't breathe even though her tank had been delivering oxygen to her lungs exactly as it was supposed to. She'd stayed under for less than ten minutes.

It wasn't enough. She needed to be under for at least a half hour, and she'd spent almost every day practicing with Nick and Ronan while Braden and Nora worked their sources for information about Manifest's next move.

"How'd it feel?" Ronan asked, treading water next to her.

"Good. I think I could have stayed down a little longer."

Nick reached a hand over the side of the boat. She reached for it and let him help her aboard, then started shedding her equipment while Ronan followed suit.

The boat swayed under her feet as she peeled off her mask and dropped her tank. They were so far out from the beach in Santorini that there was nothing but an azure stretch of sea in every direction, glittering like a blanket of diamonds under the afternoon sun.

She'd been despondent when they'd left

Florence without Elise, but the weeks in Greece had been healing. Ronan had figured out that DOS on the sheet she'd found with Elise's picture in the villa in Florence stood for Date of Sale.

Julia had been sick afterward, the idea of her sister being sold like cattle at an auction striking a new brand of terror in her body. It had made everything real. Elise's abduction had been intentional, part of a trafficking ring with so much money and power that they were sure they'd be given a free pass.

But it hadn't taken long for her fear to turn to anger. At least they knew where Elise would be next. The coordinates had pointed to the waters off the tiny Greek island of Kos, and Ronan, Julia, and Nick had promptly left for Nick's house in Greece while Declan had gone back to Boston to handle the day-to-day running of MIS and to help coordinate information with Clay and his team.

They assumed the coordinates meant the girls would be brought to one of the many multimillion-dollar yachts that routinely cruised the waters off the coast of Greece, and they'd spent hours on the boat and in the water, preparing Julia for a breach that would require them to dive to the yacht in order to avoid detection.

It had felt perverse at first — being in such a beautiful place, learning to dive like she was on vacation, walking the beaches with Ronan and wishing Chief was there with them — but she'd reminded herself again and again that it was for Elise, that this time she would not leave without her sister.

"I think I'm ready," Julia said when Ronan had shed his gear.

"I think so too." He bent to kiss her and she tasted salt on his lips. "You did good."

She knew what the words cost him, knew he didn't want to admit it, that he didn't want her to be ready for what was coming. Somewhere along the way he'd stopped arguing about whether she would come along, understanding that one way or another, she was going to look for her sister.

"Maybe we can go one more time before Saturday," she said, wanting to reassure him. "Maybe a night dive?"

His brow furrowed with worry as he unzipped his wetsuit. "Maybe."

There would be security aboard the boat carrying Elise, although they had no way of knowing how much. They wouldn't even know who the boat was registered to until it appeared at the coordinates listed on the sheet with Elise's picture.

They would have to breach it after dark, when they had a better shot at getting onboard without detection. It was always darker underwater, but so far they'd dived during the day when at least some of the sunlight managed to turn the water a soft watery blue.

It would be different the night they staged Elise's rescue, harder to keep an eye on Ronan and Nick, and on Braden, who would be diving with them while Nora stayed on the boat far enough away to avoid suspicion by the crew of the Manifest yacht but close enough to offer an assist or call in the authorities if it came to it.

They would have to play it by ear once they were on board the yacht, roll with the punches based on the number of guards and the layout of the vessel, which they hoped to get a better idea about once it moved into position. Nora had a satellite cam watching the area, waiting for it to arrive. Once it did, they would fly a drone overhead to try and get more information.

They could only hope it was far enough in advance to give them time to factor new information into their plans. It was the thing that kept Ronan up at night, the thing that forced him from their shared bed in the house on the cliff over the ocean, and she often woke to find him sitting on the terrace, his eyes frozen on the water below, like it might hold the answers to what would happen when they finally boarded the boat holding Elise.

Julia didn't try to allay his fears. That would be patronizing when his fears were all too real. Anything could happen: they might not be able to rescue Elise at all, something could happen to one of them during the rescue, none of them might make it out alive.

On those nights, she'd take the lounge chair next to him instead, reaching for his hand and sitting next to him until he was ready to return to bed. Then they would lose themselves in each other's bodies all over again, trying to forget that the hourglass on their time together might already be running out of sand.

She was pulled from her thoughts by the rumble of the boat's engine under her feet.

"Stow that gear," Nick said, lowering the dive flag. "I'm starving."

Julia shoved her tank and mask under the boat's seats and held onto one of the benches as the boat picked up speed. She looked at the water unfurling around them, wondering where Elise was at the moment. Was she out there somewhere, already aboard the yacht that would bring her to Greece? Had she given up being rescued?

Julia willed her thoughts to her sister, sending them out over the water like a message in a bottle.

I'm coming, Elise. Don't give up. I'm coming.

23

Ronan's heart dropped when he saw Nora pacing the dock as the boat slowed down on its approach. It could only be bad news if she was waiting for them: god knew they hadn't gotten a break yet.

Nick had barely cut the boat's engine when she started talking.

"There's a new boat moving into the area," she said.

Ronan tied the ropes onto the dock's cleats and stepped off the boat. "Off Kos?"

"Not yet," she said, "but it looks like that's where it's headed." She looked at Julia as Julia stepped onto the dock. "How'd the dive go?"

She'd taken to Julia like they'd been friends forever, falling into an easy camaraderie that made Ronan's heart swell. He'd been so wrapped up in his own grief after Erin's death that he hadn't thought about what it must mean for Nora to lose her only sister, to be stranded in a houseful of men without her mother or her sister, both of whom had died before their time.

No wonder she hardly ever came home to Boston. Emotionally shut down and busy with MIS, Ronan, Nick, and Declan didn't exactly give her a reason to visit.

"Good," Julia said. "I stayed under for a half hour this time."

Nora lifted her arm for a high five. "Nice."

"What makes you think the new boat is our mark?" Nick asked when he'd joined them on the dock.

They'd hacked one of the satellites for the HCG — the Hellenic Coast Guard, which was responsible for patrolling the waters off Greece — and had been watching the boats in the area since they'd arrived on Santorini. Most of them were easily traceable to wealthy owners hobnobbing in the area and were gone within a few days of their first sighting.

"I ran the registration when I saw it heading for Kos," Nora said. "It's shady."

"Shady how?" Ronan asked.

"Shady like all the other stuff surrounding Manifest. Shell companies leading to shell companies leading to shell companies. No clear owner."

"Could be a legitimate someone looking for privacy," Nick said.

"Could be," Nora agreed. "But we're four days out from Saturday, so I figured it's worth keeping an eye on."

Four days until the date listed on the asset sheet with Elise's picture that Julia had found at the villa in Florence. Four days until he had no choice but to let Julia walk back into the lion's den with the sick fucks of Manifest.

It felt even more dangerous than the villa in Florence. He tried to tell himself it was because of the close call: his and Julia's flight underground, the alarm squealing in the villa, the quick getaway with Nick at the wheel. He even told himself it was the location of their next mission, the yacht and the fact that there would be nowhere to run, no tunnel to provide an escape, just miles and miles of sea.

But it was all a lie, or a distraction at best. The real problem was Julia. If Elise was on the boat, Julia wouldn't leave without her, even if it meant sacrificing her own life.

And Ronan had a feeling that this time, Elise would be there.

They couldn't even begin to plan a way onto the boat until they knew what kind of boat it was, and even then, getting a handle on security would be next to impossible at this late date. It meant the whole job was a powder keg of potential problems, the very last kind of place he wanted Julia to be.

But he'd given up trying to convince her not to come along. She'd fought him every step of the way so far, and he had no reason to believe this would be any different. The fact that she knew how to fire a weapon gave him only modest comfort. Beyond that, he could only hope to keep her close, get Elise, and get the hell out as quickly as possible.

On his best days, he thought the operation in Greece might be the beginning of the end of the barrier between them. On those days he was hopeful that they would rescue Elise and bring her back to Boston. Julia would see that he still loved her, that what they had wasn't just a product of Elise's disappearance.

That it was real.

Other times he wasn't so sure. He would catch Julia looking out to sea, her eyes shadowed with thoughts she didn't want to share, and he'd wonder if she would ever fully trust in his love.

And there was another fear, one that lurked in

the deepest recesses of his mind, one he didn't dare speak aloud: that Julia would feel she owed him if they rescued Elise. That once they brought Elise home, he would never truly know if she loved him or if she was repaying a debt.

He'd tried in vain to break down the last remaining wall between them during their weeks in Greece, but it was still there, invisible to the eye but as impenetrable as granite. His desire to turn it to rubble was starting to feel like a mandate, the only way he'd be sure she loved him if they managed to rescue Elise.

June 25th was only four days away.

Four days to identify the boat carrying Elise and come up with a plan.

Four days to destroy the wall Julia had spent a lifetime building between her and the world, the one she'd spent months maintaining between them.

It wasn't enough time.

24

"What can I do?" Julia asked Nora, standing at the counter in the kitchen, laying out crumbly chunks of feta, stuffed grape leaves, and olives on a platter.

Nora smiled up at her and Julia was struck again by her eyes, as clear and blue as Ronan's. "Nothing. You've been in the water all day. You must be wiped."

Julia smiled. "I'm fine. I can help."

Nora turned to the fridge and removed a six pack of beer. "You can take these to the terrace and put them in the ice chest."

"That's it?"

"That's it. Seriously, I've been inside most of the day running the registration on that Oceanco. I'm happy to be busy."

Nora had explained on the way up to the house

that the boat picked up by the satellite heading for Kos was a three-hundred-foot Oceanco yacht.

"Let me know if you change your mind," Julia said, taking the beer and heading to the terrace.

She'd been surprised by how much she liked Nora Murphy, surprised by how natural their friendship felt. After living in close quarters with Elise her entire life, Julia knew she missed her sister, but she hadn't realized how much she'd missed the companionship of another woman, especially in the testosterone-fueled Murphy house.

Nora was quick to call the men on their shit — Braden included — and just as quick to ruffle their hair like they were still little boys even though they all loomed over her. It was clear they adored her, and equally clear that the vacuum left by Erin's death was still present, a jagged, invisible hole everyone stepped carefully around.

"Anyone need another beer?" Julia asked as she stepped onto the terrace.

Nick stood over the grill, brushing tuna steaks with olive oil and squeezing lemon over them while Braden and Ronan sat around a laptop at the other end of the patio, looking at the satellite images of the Oceanco yacht.

"I'll take one," Nick said.

She handed him one of the bottles and took one for herself, then bent to put the rest in the cooler on the ground near the grill.

"Those smell amazing," she said, looking at the tuna.

"Fishmonger said they were caught this morning," Nick said. "It's one of the things I love most about this place."

She took in the sweeping views of the Aegean sea, the white stucco houses stark against their blue tiled roofs and the water that surrounded everything. "It must be one of a million."

He smiled. "You have a point."

"Do you come here often?" she asked.

He sprinkled salt on the tuna. "When I can get away. It's like another world here. All the things I worry about in Boston don't seem to matter."

She wondered what Nick Murphy worried about in Boston but didn't want to pry. "I can see that."

He looked more closely at her. "How are you holding up?"

"I'm okay." She looked down at the beer in her hand. "It's hard to feel like I deserve to enjoy anything."

"I felt that way," he said. "After Erin."

She nodded. "I'm sorry."

"It took me a long time to believe that Erin would want me to keep living." He shrugged, but the nonchalance felt forced. "But that's different than with Elise."

"How so?"

"Erin was dead. Of course she would want me to live. What else could I do?" he hesitated. "You must feel like you shouldn't be doing anything but trying to find her."

"Pretty much," she admitted. "I know it's not possible. I'm a person. I need to sleep and eat, and I'm limited to what I can do at any given moment."

"But this isn't a situation where intellect rules," Nick pointed out.

"Exactly. I keep wondering if she's hurt or scared, if she thinks I've given up on her." Despair rose in her throat like bile. She shook her head. "I try not to think about those things, but it's hard."

He didn't say anything for a long time, testing the fish with a fork to see if it was done. "I used to obsess over Erin's last moments. I'd play out all the different scenarios — she knew what was happening to her and wanted someone to save her, she fell asleep and never knew what happened to her, she was scared, in pain..." He shook his head. "It's a kind of hell."

"How did you stop?" she asked.

He looked at her and she was struck by his eyes, not blue like Ronan's, but green like the leaves on the old trees surrounding her gramps' property. "Honestly?"

She nodded.

"I just played it out. Eventually, I'd imagined everything so many times that it didn't have as much power over me. And in the end, she was still gone."

The resignation in his voice terrified her. She knew it was different: Erin was dead — there was still hope of saving Elise.

But it was all too easy to imagine herself someday telling a story like this one, a story where Elise was gone and nothing would ever, ever bring her back.

"I think it was hardest on Ronan," Nick said.

Julia glanced at Ronan, his head tipped toward something Braden was pointing out on the laptop, then returned her eyes to Nick. "Why do you say that?"

She knew Erin's death had broken Ronan, that it had driven him in some way toward every decision he'd made since, but she was surprised to hear Nick say it had been hardest on him.

"He's the oldest," Nick said. "It wasn't just implied that it was his job to look out for us — my dad used to say it." He affected a deeper voice, mimicking his father. "*Ronan, look out for your sisters. Are you going to let someone bully your little brothers, Ronan? Don't just stand there, Ronan, do something. If you don't look out for them, who will?*"

"That's a lot of pressure," Julia said.

"I don't think he really felt it until Erin started using." He smiled. "In fact, I'd say before that he actually enjoyed being the overlord."

Julia smiled. "It has its advantages."

Nick nodded. "But when Erin OD'ed, Ronan took it personally. In his eyes, he'd failed her, had failed us all."

"Which is why he started MIS." Julia knew Ronan had been the one to start the business, although to hear him tell it, it hadn't taken much to convince Nick and Declan to join him.

Nick raised his beer in assent, then grew quiet as he started pulling the tuna off the grill. "He's been different these past few months you've been around."

"Different?"

"He hasn't been quite as much of an asshole." Nick laughed a little before his expression grew serious. "I think maybe he's started to believe that something good could happen for him again, but like you, he feels guilty that it's come at your sister's expense."

"We didn't exactly meet under normal circumstances," she said. "Everything's been upside down since the beginning."

Nick closed the grill and turned his eyes on her. She wasn't prepared for the worry she saw there.

"Thing is, I'm not sure he'd make it through another mind fuck."

She blinked, surprised to hear Nick use the figure of speech. "I'm not fucking with him."

"I'm not implying it's intentional," he said. "But I know this is a difficult time for you — believe me, I know — and it can make it hard to think about how it affects the people around you." Her face grew hot, and she opened her mouth to defend herself only to have Nick hold up a hand to stop her. "I'm just doing my due diligence for my brother. He's head over heels for you, Julia. It's a lot of power to have over someone. I just want to make sure you know you're wielding it, whether you want it or not, and that you're being straight with him."

She wanted to protest, to say of course she was being straight with Ronan. That she loved him, that she'd told him she loved him and meant it.

But the words rang hollow because deep down

she knew Nick's warning had been issued for a reason. She'd been holding something back from Ronan since the beginning, that tiny part of herself that worried what they had was like a comet, an anomaly born out of Elise's disappearance that wouldn't hold up under the weight of everyday life.

She'd told herself it was because of Ronan. That he was a danger junkie, a man who would never be happy with one woman, a man who would never be satisfied coming home to sit around the dinner table with a wife and kids when bad guys were still running around waiting to be caught. That their relationship worked because it was conducted within the confines of the danger that was a part of his life.

But that was a cop-out. The truth was she was scared. Scared of her own ability to stick it out, to do what her mother had never done and build a life with someone that was built on something solid.

Something real.

Deep down she wondered if maybe she was her mother's daughter after all, less flighty than Elise on the surface but every bit as weak.

Nick picked up the platter of fish and smiled. Any anger she'd felt dissipated. Nick was looking out for his family. She'd done the same a hundred times for Elise.

"I like you," he said. "It's been awesome having you around, and I hope you'll stay. But if you don't plan to, it would be better for Ronan if you told him sooner rather than later."

25

Ronan spread the blueprint out across the table on the terrace and used the salt and pepper shakers, a napkin holder, and Nick's empty bottle of beer to hold down the corners.

"This is the Oceanco LR 100," he said. The blueprints illustrated two views of the yacht, the exterior measurements and the interior layout. "It can carry a crew of up to thirty-one, plus twenty-two passengers at one time."

"A crew of thirty-one?" Julia repeated. "How many of those will be security guards?"

"We don't know," Ronan said. "There's a lot we don't know, but we'll go over that in a second. You should all take a mental snapshot of the ship's interior, because we'll need to move fast once we're inside."

They'd come to the conclusion that the Oceanco vessel named Elysium was the boat that belonged to Manifest when it moved into position over the exact coordinates listed on Elise's asset sheet in Florence. It had been anchored there for the past two days and showed no sign of leaving.

Tomorrow was June 25th.

"You can see the primary lounge area here." He pointed to a large open space at the craft's stern. "Not ideal, because it means we'll have to board the ship from the bow to avoid detection."

"Is that even possible?" Julia asked. When they dived, they dropped off the side or rear of the boat, but they were always pulled back aboard at the stern, which sat lower in the water.

"It's possible," Nick said. "We'll have to throw up a line and rappel up, but it's doable."

"We just have to make sure we aren't spotted before we're on board," Braden said.

"That'll be the hard part," Ronan agreed, "especially since we don't know more about security."

The satellite imagery had helped, showing a rotating series of guards patrolling the deck of the Elysium, but the images didn't tell them anything about the total number of guards on board, or about other security measures like cameras or alarms.

"Someone will have to surface and get a look before you board," Nora said. "It's not foolproof but if you take a minute, you should be able to get a sense of the timing of the patrol."

Nora had agreed to stay in the boat that would act as their dive point. They needed somebody who could work the satellite feeds in order to know if and when she should call the authorities for help, and they needed someone who was ready to drive the boat once they got Elise onboard.

If they got Elise on board.

"It's not ideal," Braden said.

"No," Ronan agreed, "but it's all we have."

"Twenty-two passengers doesn't allow for a lot of guests," Julia said.

Ronan nodded. "The assumption is that the auction is online."

"So the boat will only carry crew, security, the women, and a handful of people running the auction for Manifest," Nick said.

"That's what I'm guessing." Ronan hated that he was guessing about any of it. Guessing got people killed, and this time guessing could get Julia killed.

But this was their last chance. The Elysium was in position ahead of the date of sale listed on Elise's asset sheet. Once she was taken off the yacht, the chances of ever finding her again were slim at best.

"At least we don't have to worry about a bunch of rich fucks wandering the deck with champagne," Nick said.

Ronan turned his attention to the interior view of the boat. "These are the cabins." He tapped the blueprints where they showed bedrooms. "This is probably where Elise will be kept, and any of the other women if they're there."

"What do we do about them?" Julia asked. "The other women."

It was a question Ronan had been dreading. "Getting Elise out alive is our mission."

"We can't just leave the other women there," Julia said.

"And hopefully we won't have to," Ronan said. "But we have to remember that getting Elise is our objective. We do what we can for the other women, but not at Elise's expense."

He ignored the voice in his head that said he would never be able to leave the other victims behind. Those were the kinds of decisions he made on the fly, when he had no one to worry about but himself.

Risking Julia's life — and Elise's, if they were finally in sight of saving it — wasn't an option.

He could see the internal war playing out on Julia's features, knew that she wouldn't go quietly if it meant leaving behind other women, but it wasn't something he could worry about right now.

"Will we have comms once we get to the boat?" Nick asked.

"We'll have comms with each other," Ronan said. "Not with Nora. She'll be anchored too far away from the Elysium." He looked at his sister, glad at least one of the two women who meant the world to him would be safe from harm during their breach of the Elysium. "You'll have to keep tabs via the satellite feed."

"How will I know when to call for help?" Nora was a professional, a seasoned former FBI agent who had an additional four years experience working for Locke Montgomery, but calling in help meant legal exposure for MIS.

There would be questions about who they were and what they were doing there. Those questions could lead to criminal charges, but if it meant getting Julia and Elise out alive, Ronan would accept whatever came, even the end of the business he'd built with his brothers.

Even prison.

"Use your best judgement," Ronan said. "The mission's objective is to get Elise out alive." He hoped his sister heard Julia's name as an unspoken addition. "If it looks like that mission can't be accomplished without assistance, call them in."

"That's putting me in a tough spot, Ro," Nora said.

"I trust you."

She looked at Nick, a question in her eyes.

Nick nodded. "At least if we go down, we take them with us."

She turned to Braden, who sighed.

"Fuck it," he said. "These bastards deserve to be destroyed."

"It's a last resort," Ronan clarified. "But do it if you have to."

"What's the plan once we're on the boat?" Nick asked.

"You and Braden take point on the guards," Ronan said. "Keep them as clear of Julia and me as possible while we look for Elise. We'll want to get off the Elysium as quickly as possible, so once we have her, we take one of the two motorboats." He tapped the Elysium where the lifeboats were suspended. "Here or here."

"We should get rid of the one we don't use," Braden said.

Ronan nodded. "No reason to make it easy for anyone to come after us." He looked around the table. "Any questions?"

Julia met his gaze and the steadiness in her eyes sent an arrow of dread into his stomach. He wanted her to be scared, to understand the danger she was assuming in boarding the Elysium. Then at least she might be careful, weigh the risks of her movements aboard the boat against the potential of a positive outcome.

But he saw only clear-eyed resolve, a determination he'd come to know well over the past few months. It was determination that said she would do whatever it took, that she would look past fear and even common sense to see something done.

It was a look that said she wasn't afraid, and that scared him most of all.

26

Julia looked around the table at the people laughing and drinking, the people who had come to mean so much to her over the previous weeks and months, and felt a swell of gratitude. Braden and Nora were laughing over something, their heads tipped together. Julia enjoyed watching them, their movements synchronized in a way that spoke to their history not only as lovers, but as friends and colleagues.

Ronan's hand rested on Julia's thigh, but his attention was on Nick, who was recounting a story from their childhood, the details of which were being hotly but laughingly debated between the two brothers.

Nora paused from her conversion with Braden to

insert her version of the story, uniting the brothers against her recollection.

Over the previous weeks, they'd become her friends, and in a way, her family.

They'd been sitting at the beachside restaurant for the past three hours, drinking cold beer and ouzo and eating an array of delicious food that included octopus salad, fried clams, and crusty bread dipped in olive oil sprinkled with fresh rosemary and sea salt.

They might have been on holiday, five friends, taking a break from their busy lives to eat and dive and lay in the sun, except tomorrow at this time they would be on a boat headed for the open water of the Aegean. Nora would park it far enough away that it wouldn't set off alarm bells for the crew of the Elysium, and Julia, Ronan, Nick, and Braden would don their diving gear and plunge into the dark waters, then swim toward the yacht that was Elise's prison.

It was possible not all of them would make it out alive.

It was possible none of them would.

Guilt rolled through her body like a wave and she had to ball her fists together in her lap to keep her hands from shaking. All of the people around the table were risking their lives for her, for Elise.

She had the sudden desire to call it all off, to tell them it had all been a terrible mistake, they should let the police do their job and hope for the best.

But she knew she wouldn't do that.

The police weren't doing their job, and Elise was too well hidden — hidden by power and wealth and a brotherhood whose bond was victimization — for anyone to find her within the bounds of the law.

The people around the table had made their choice. Elise hadn't had one, but that didn't make it any easier to know that someone else might get hurt — or worse.

She stood and forced a smile. She needed a minute. Needed to get away from the smiling faces of the people she'd come to love, of the people who were willing to risk everything for her and her sister.

They'd made a lie of everything Julia had believed, of everything she'd told herself she believed, anyway. That people were inherently selfish, that they always looked out for themselves first, that you had to look out for yourself too, because no one else was going to do it for you.

"Excuse me." She left her napkin on her chair and

made her way through the small group of people on the restaurant's beachside patio, trying not to think about the silence that had descended around the table.

Tonight of all nights, Ronan, Nick, Braden, and Nora deserved to have fun.

Stepping around the rope that marked the restaurant's dining area, she continued onto the beach, her feet sinking into the sand as she made her way toward the darkened waterline.

The sun had gone down over an hour ago, but it was still warm, the breeze a caress against her shoulders, bare under her sleeveless blouse. She waited until she'd stepped out of the light cast from the restaurant to take off her shoes, the soft clatter of silverware and murmur of conversation falling behind her like a shadow.

She inhaled the briny scent of the ocean and walked through the shallow surf rolling onto the beach, Ronan's face as she'd stood from the table fresh in her mind. She'd wanted to smooth the worry from his brow, to apologize for causing him to risk everything on a job even Nick must think was a fool's mission.

She thought about her conversation with Nick on the terrace two days earlier, a conversation that hadn't been far from her mind since. If he knew she was holding something back from Ronan, Ronan must feel it too.

Sorrow squeezed her heart in a vise. She'd thought her fear of the future, her doubt about the foundation of their relationship, had been private. She hadn't wanted Ronan to see it, but now she saw that that was the most foolish thing of all.

He saw everything.

She'd been a coward, hiding behind the wall she'd started building when she was a little girl, each brick carefully laid, a barrier against the kind of pain she'd seen her mother suffer time and again, a hedge against ever giving herself fully to someone, a self-fulfilling prophecy that would guarantee no one ever got close enough to really know and love her.

Except Ronan had gotten close enough. He did know and love her, and somehow his love had made cracks in her precious wall.

"Julia!"

She turned toward the sound of his voice and saw him making his way toward her in the dark.

"Hey," he said when he caught up. He placed his hands on her shoulders. "You okay?"

"I'm sorry. I just... I needed to walk."

"Don't be sorry." He took her hand. "Want company?"

She nodded and they continued along the beach. The surf rolled over Julia's feet, the water warm on her skin.

"I feel bad," she confessed. "About tomorrow."

"What do you mean?"

"Just… everyone risking their lives, their freedom, for me, for Elise."

"It's our choice," Ronan said. "And it's what we do, all of us."

She didn't know the details of Braden and Nora's work with Locke Montgomery, but she'd gathered that they worked with similar goals as MIS using very different methods.

"I know, but I can't help feeling responsible."

He stopped walking and took her face in his hands. His eyes were dark and unreadable as he looked down at her.

"Don't," he said. "With or without you and Elise, none of us would be able to leave this alone now that we know about Manifest."

"I keep wanting to say thank you, but thank you seems so small," she confessed.

She was surprised to see something like anger flash across his features. He stepped away, running his hands through his hair.

"What is it?" she asked. "What did I say?"

He turned to face her. "You don't have to thank me, Julia. Thanks is for a casserole someone brings over when you have a death in the family, for a ride from a friend when your car's broken down."

She turned her hands toward the sky. "I don't know what else to say."

He walked toward her, his eyes blazing, stopping when he was so close she could feel the heat of his body. "Don't say anything. You're my family, Julia. I'd do anything for you. Don't you know that?"

She swallowed around the lump in her throat. "I do."

"Then why are you so determined to hold yourself apart from me?"

She opened her mouth to deny it, then thought better of it. Ronan didn't deserve lies.

"I don't know," she said quietly. "I guess I'm scared."

"Of me?"

She shook her head. "Of myself."

He reached down and tucked a piece of windblown hair behind her ear. "Help me understand."

"I've never seen two people love each other in a way that was anything other than toxic." She'd been young when her grandmother died, too young to view her marriage to Julia's gramps through the lens of adulthood. "I've never seen a woman love a man without losing herself."

"Those women aren't you, Julia. Those men aren't me."

She nodded. "It's just hard to let go."

"We're all scared. Every one of us. But Julia..." He shook his head. "I won't settle for part of you. I can't. Not when I'm giving you everything."

"I want to give you everything too." There were other words stuck in her throat, words she'd wanted to say since her conversation with Nick, words she'd wanted to say since long before that, but this was all she could manage. "I'm just I'm not sure how to do it."

He pulled her into his arms and looked down at her. "Just let go."

His voice was hoarse and he lowered his mouth to hers, sweeping her into a kiss with so much urgency it stole her breath. It was a kiss that said he was done waiting, a kiss that said he'd burn down anything between them with the force of his love.

She slid her arms around his neck and pressed her body against his, molding herself to every sculpted peak and valley until there was no space for anything else.

By the time she broke away, she was on fire, heat

radiating outward from her belly, her underwear wet with her desire, her body clamoring for him to fill her.

"Take me to bed, Ronan."

He pulled her against his side and hurried up the beach.

There was peace in surrender.

27

The house was quiet when they returned, everyone else still at the restaurant on the beach. His hands were roaming her body before he'd even closed the door behind them.

A breeze blew through the open terrace doors as they made their way through the house, their kisses growing more frenzied as they crossed the living room and made their way down the hall to the room that was theirs while they were in Greece.

There was no tenderness in his kiss. He'd used up all his tenderness in the months she'd been withholding from him, the months he'd done everything in his power to get her to let go.

Now all he had was his hunger for her.

They were on the threshold to the bedroom when she reached for the hem of his T-shirt. She pulled it over his head, her fingers traveling over his chest as he unfastened the buttons of her blouse, kissing his way across her silky shoulder as he slid the fabric off her arms.

She smelled like coconut, vanilla, and the sea and he inhaled her scent like it might be the one thing to save him.

The room was bathed in moonlight, the sheer curtains billowing around the open doors. He cradled her face in his hands as he led her to the bed.

"Nothing between us this time, Julia."

He knelt at her feet and unbuttoned her jeans, then slid them from her legs along with her underwear. She stepped out of them and he looked up at her body, a refuge from everything ugly in the world.

She was the most beautiful thing he'd ever seen.

He kissed his way up the inside of her thigh, letting his lips sink into the plush flesh, inhaling the musky scent of her sex as he drew closer to the cleft between her thighs.

She sighed and slipped her hands into his hair.

"You thought I wouldn't know," he murmured, closing his mouth over her sex through the thin fabric of her panties. "You thought it was enough to give me your body."

She gasped. "Yes."

His cock strained against the confines of his jeans, begging for her paradise.

"No more," he said softly, pulling her underwear aside.

He ran his tongue through her soaking folds and his shaft got harder still as she let out a long moan.

He lifted his face from her pussy and her fingers tightened in his hair. The sensation sent a powerful surge of desire to the tip of his cock. "Tell me there will never be anything between us again."

She looked down at him, her eyes hooded with the weight of her desire. "Never."

"Never what?" He wanted to hear her say it.

The haze in her eyes cleared. "There will never be anything between us again."

He tugged the underwear off her body and buried his face between her legs, plunging his tongue into her channel as he worked her clit with his thumb.

"Oh my god…" she breathed.

He lapped at her juices like a man dying of thirst, covering her sex with his mouth, teasing her clit until it grew as hard and swollen as a spring bud under his tongue.

She was already close to coming. He could feel it

in the coil of her body, the rhythmic motion of her hips matching the motion of his mouth as he licked her pussy.

He stood and raked his teeth over one of her lace-covered nipples, then sucked it until it grew to a hard peak under her bra.

She dropped her head back. "Ronan…"

He reached behind her, unhooked the bra, and tossed it aside, savoring the feel of her warm skin against his chest.

She reached for the button of his jeans and he closed his mouth over hers, sweeping it with his tongue as she worked his zipper.

Lust tore through his body when she closed her hand around the shaft of his cock and he nudged her back onto the bed and pulled off his jeans, eager to feel her stretched out underneath him.

He stood over the bed and looked down at her, wanting to memorize the way the moonlight streamed in through the open doors, bathing her body in pearly light. Her breasts were full, her nipples jutting hard and pink, begging for his mouth. Her waist narrowed to a soft belly. He knew exactly how it would feel when he nipped at the pillowy flesh with his teeth, knew that it would be like silk under his cheek.

The hair between her legs was fair, her legs long and muscular, tapering to strong calves and shapely feet that he could almost feel on his shoulders as he drove into her.

She lifted her arms, reaching for him, and he turned toward the nightstand for a condom.

"No," she said.

He looked at her. "No?"

"Nothing between us tonight," she said. "Remember?"

A knot of emotion in his chest made it hard for him to breathe. "Are you sure?"

"I'm sure," she said. "Come here."

He stretched out over her body and kissed her, slanting his mouth over hers to take their kiss deeper, wanting to take up residence inside every hidden corner in the secret garden of her body.

She arched her back, meeting the urgency of his kiss with a demand of her own, pulling her knees up around his hips so that his shaft nestled into the wet heat between her legs, a tease of the nirvana that was to come.

He kissed his way across her jaw, up her cheekbones and over her closed eyelids. Her breath was a whisper across his skin and he touched his lips behind her ear and down her neck, lingering over the pronounced well of her collarbone before turning his attention to the erect buds of her nipples.

He closed his lips around one of them and her fingers found their way into his hair as he tongued the peak, sucking until she moaned.

He cupped the breast in his hand, rolling the dusty pink nipple, wet from his mouth, between his fingers as he took the other one between his lips. Her body writhed under his, her hips lifting off the bed in a silent plea.

Her need stoked his own, and his cock throbbed against her silken sex, so close that he could be inside her with one thrust. He let his engorged tip brush against her clit, relishing the way she tried to position her hips under his to force him inside her.

When he couldn't stand it a second longer he knelt between her legs and positioned his cock at her entrance.

Her body was laid out like a feast, chest flushed with pleasure, nipples wet and thrusting into the air. The soft curls covering her mound were damp, moisture beading on the petals of her sex, her thighs spread for him.

He pushed into her with a slow, hard thrust, tunneling through her enveloping softness until he came to a stop against the barrier of her cervix.

She gasped, her nails digging into his back, and wrapped her legs around his waist until he sank deeper.

"Nothing between us." Her eyes blazed amber fire. "Not this time. Not ever again."

The words were kerosene on the fire of his passion and he moved inside her, pulling out and driving into her again, watching her face as he occupied every inch of her body.

He wanted to go slow, to savor the moment when they were finally one, but he could feel her climbing toward climax, could feel it in the tightening of her pussy as it clamped down on his shaft, the urgency in her hips as she rose to meet him.

"I'm going to come, Ronan," she gasped.

He didn't want her to hold back. He didn't want her to ever hold anything back again.

"Come for me, beautiful."

She cried out into the room, her body shuddering under his, and his own release took hold.

He pushed through her swollen channel, thrusting again and again, pouring himself into her until they were both panting and spent, until he knew for sure there was nothing more between them.

28

Ronan was asleep when Julia slipped out of bed. They'd heard Nick, Braden, and Nora come in at some point in the night, but neither of them had wanted to break the spell of their time alone. They'd lain in bed, laughing softly so no one would hear and hoping everyone would think they were asleep. Then they'd made love again, this time slowly and quietly, like they were both trying to memorize every moment in case it was their last.

She put on Ronan's shirt and slipped onto the terrace off the bedroom. The moon was just a crescent, but the sky was so clear it lit up the sea below.

She looked past the boats docked in the marina, her eyes on the horizon. She knew Elise was out there, could feel her sister's presence. Could Elise see the moon from a window onboard the Elysium?

Did she know she was off the coast of Greece? Did she know what was about to happen to her?

It didn't matter. At this time tomorrow night, it would all be over. Either they would have Elise or they wouldn't. Either they would make it out alive, or they wouldn't.

She walked herself through the night ahead: the boat that would take them into position, the night dive to the Elysium, their breach of the yacht, the moment when she and Ronan would split off from Braden and Nick, their search of the cabins for Elise.

She knew she was the weak link in the team, the one with no experience, but she was determined not to be a liability. Like everyone else, she would be armed, and she wouldn't hesitate to use her weapon if it meant saving her sister, if it meant saving any of them.

She'd avoided calling her grandfather with an update since Florence. She wanted the next call she made to him to be the one where she told him Elise was safe and sound. False hope was too hard to bear, and he'd borne more than his share of it since their trip to Dubai.

She imagined her and Elise back at her gramps' house, sitting on the deck while he grilled steaks, both of them wrapped in one of his old blankets and drinking homemade lemonade while he told them about his latest strongly worded letter to the editor of the local newspaper.

The moment felt both impossible and close enough to touch.

"Hey." Ronan's hands came down on her shoulders. He kissed her neck and a shiver ran up her spine. "You okay?"

She turned in his arms and nodded, then touched her lips to his. "I'm sorry if I woke you."

"Don't be. I don't want to sleep without you."

A few weeks ago the words would have terrified her. They would have felt like a jinx on an already precarious situation. Now she knew her relationship with Ronan had never been precarious: it had only been her faith in herself that had been shaky, and that had been nothing but an old story she'd told so many times that she'd believed it without question when it had been flawed all along.

"I don't want to sleep without you either." He pulled her closer and she looked up at him, thinking about where they would be the following night. "Is it going to be okay?"

It was something she wouldn't have dared ask a few weeks earlier. She'd been holding her doubts close, not wanting them to seep into the consciousness of Ronan or Nick or Declan, wanting them to believe she was a hundred percent certain they were going to find Elise, get her out alive, make it out alive themselves.

"Nothing between us?" he asked.

"Nothing."

"I don't know," he said. "But I will promise you one thing."

"Okay." A promise from Ronan was one she could take to the bank. Whatever it was, she would cling to it with both hands.

"Whatever happens tomorrow night, I won't rest until whoever did this pays, one way or another."

She tightened her arms around him and rested her cheek against his bare chest.

His words should have given her comfort. Instead they had the hint of a bad omen. She couldn't help feeling that it was too good to be true — setting things right with Ronan, getting Elise out alive, going about her life like she was a normal person, a person who deserved happiness.

Believing it was harder than it should have been.

29

Ronan checked a stack of ammo before setting it into the black duffel on the terrace. He was checking the ammo while Nick did a last-minute check of the weapons and Braden inventoried the grenades and other supplies.

They'd been working quietly for the past half hour, each of them checking off boxes in their mental checklists that would ensure they were prepared for anything. The supply check was soothing and Ronan was glad when Nora had convinced Julia to spend an hour on the beach. He'd been able to feel Julia's tension, to see it in the way she held her body too tight, her spine straight enough to snap while she paced the house.

It was a reminder of all that was at stake, a reminder that she was inexperienced, that as much as the Elysium was a wild card, Julia was one too, and her own safety was the biggest thing at stake.

"Something you want to say?"

He glanced up to find Nick's eyes on him. Braden was still working, counting out tear gas grenades and setting them in the duffel, but Ronan wasn't fooled. Braden would be listening to every word.

Ronan sat back on his heels. Having siblings who knew you so well was a blessing and a curse.

"I want you to promise to get her out," he said.

Nick's jaw was set, his eyes hard. "That's the idea."

"You know what I mean," Ronan said.

"Maybe you should spell it out," Nick said.

"I want you to get Julia out no matter what."

Nick held his gaze. "No matter what?"

"No matter what." Ronan was going to leave it at that but decided to make it crystal clear, just to make sure there wouldn't be any room for Nick to squirm out of it later. "If you have to leave me behind, leave me behind. If you have to sacrifice me, sacrifice me. But whatever happens, you get Julia out alive."

"That's the mission now?" It wasn't really a question.

"That's the mission. In a perfect world, we get

Elise too. But the prime directive is to get Julia out alive," Ronan said.

Nick set down the semiautomatic weapon in his hand and stood. "So this isn't a rescue mission anymore. It's an exercise for Julia."

Ronan stood, unfurling himself to his full height until he was looking down slightly at his younger brother. "It's a rescue mission with a caveat: if the rescue means sacrificing Julia, we abort."

"At any cost?" There was a challenge in Nick's eyes.

"At any cost."

"Jesus..." Nick turned away, running his hands through his hair before turning back to face Ronan with his eyes blazing. "Are you sure you're thinking with the head on top of your neck?"

Ronan's voice was low. "I'm going to pretend you didn't say that."

"It's an honest question," Nick said.

They stared each other down, Ronan's fist balled at his sides as he tried to reign in his temper.

Braden was still kneeling on the terrace, pretending he wasn't bearing witness to the argument.

Ronan looked at his brother, trying to think of something he could say to make Nick understand.

Something that would make it clear that Ronan had thought it through, that he knew exactly what he was doing, that he would do it a hundred times over if it meant keeping Julia safe.

Nick flinched when Ronan clasped a hand on his shoulder, like his brother had expected to take a fist to the jaw.

He looked in his brother's eyes. "I love her."

Nick held his gaze so long Ronan wondered if he'd registered the words.

Finally he raised his hands as if in surrender, exhaling like he'd been holding his breath for a hundred years. "Fine. Fuck it. Whatever you say, Ro."

Ronan pulled his brother into an embrace and clapped him on the back. Nick stiffened like he was surprised before leaning into the hug. Ronan couldn't remember the last time they'd embraced.

"Thank you."

30

Julia held onto the bench underneath her as the boat sped across dark waters. Ronan stood silently next to her, bracing himself on the back of the bench while Braden stood next to Nora, steering the boat.

Nick sat apart, silent and brooding, and Julia wondered what had happened while she'd been at the beach with Nora. They'd returned to find the men packing the last of their supplies, the tension so thick it was almost visible.

Nora had waved off her raised eyebrows. "They'll get over it, whatever it is."

Other than her gramps and her mother's assorted boyfriends and husbands, Julia hadn't spent a lot of time around men, especially those with as close and complicated a relationship as the Murphy brothers. She'd kept quiet, figuring Ronan would talk if he felt like it. They'd spent the rest of the afternoon and evening going over last minute details gleaned from the latest satellite footage of the Elysium.

They were almost positive the security detail involved two guards patrolling the deck, one at the stern and one at the back, plus one on the bridge. Julia had been surprised there weren't more of them, but Ronan had reminded her there were likely more belowdeck.

Still, she'd felt a burst of optimism. The plan for boarding the Elysium relied on their ability to board the craft from the bow, and that meant surfacing long enough to hook a line that could be used to climb up from the water.

One guard at the front seemed manageable.

She'd played out every possible scenario for freeing Elise once they found her in one of the cabins, but she knew it wasn't enough. There were a million things she couldn't anticipate, and there was no way out but through.

Ronan reached for her hand and squeezed and she turned to find him looking at her. He didn't say anything — it would be impossible to hear him over the roar of the wind and the boat's engine — but she saw the fear in his eyes.

It was what pained her most: knowing she'd caused such a fearless man, a warrior in every sense of the word, to be afraid. She was surprised he didn't hate her for that, hoped he wouldn't come to in the long run.

The boat slowed to a crawl, the noise gradually lessening as the boat came to a stop.

Ronan squeezed her hand, stood, and moved to drop the anchor.

The boat bobbed in the water and Nick moved up to the digital display on the boat's dashboard.

"Is that it?" he asked, pointing to a green shadow on the screen.

"That's it," said Nora. "Mark the coordinates and set your GPS."

Nick would be their navigator, leading them through the water to the Elysium approximately half a mile away. Braden would follow behind him, then Julia, then Ronan.

Julia looked over the side of the boat and was relieved to see that the water was calm. They'd done a practice night dive two nights before and it had been more disorienting than she'd expected. She was confident she could follow Nick and Braden — and Ronan would be behind her to keep her on track — but dealing with rough waters at the same time was a challenge she had hoped not to face.

Braden reached for his tank. "Let's suit up."

Julia zipped up her wetsuit and started putting on the rest of her gear while Nick and Ronan did the same.

"Check your air," Ronan reminded her.

She put on her mask and took a breath. The sound of air moving through the hoses was reassuring.

She could do this.

She held up a thumb and Ronan signaled for her to turnaround so he could check the levels on her tank and make sure the hoses were securely attached. It was a precaution he didn't make with anyone else, but she wouldn't fight it if it made him feel better. She was new enough to diving that the added security made her feel better too.

They lined up at the back of the boat.

"Check your comms," Nora said.

They went through an audio check, each of them reporting in with their name. Julia wondered if their voices would sound as clear once they were underwater.

"I'll keep the sat feed up as long as I can," Nora

said. "If it looks like you're in trouble, I'll either come for you myself or I'll send help."

Braden lifted his mask. "Send help."

Nora's eyes hardened and Julia got a glimpse of the tug-of-war that must go hand in hand with working in a dangerous field with your significant other. "You do your job, I'll do mine."

Braden glared at Nora and replaced his mask.

She looked at each of them. "Ready?"

They nodded and she turned to Nick and held up three fingers.

3... 2... 1.

Nick went over the side and Nora held up a hand, waiting a few seconds before she gave a similar countdown to Braden.

Julia waited for Braden to move away from the drop zone at the back of the boat, then looked at Ronan. She wanted to tell him she would be okay, that this would all be over soon, but there was no time.

Nora held up her fingers. Julia forced herself to breathe.

Then she was tipping over the side of the boat, the water closing in over her head as she sank through the muffled abyss.

31

Ronan didn't dare look at his dive watch as they swam through the dark. He was too focused on Julia in front of him, too worried about losing sight of her.

Like all of them, she wore a clip light that illuminated her position, a beacon of gold that made it easier for him to keep his eyes on her, but he was all too aware of the vastness of the water around them. It would only take a few seconds for one of them to disappear.

He didn't know how long they'd been swimming when Nick's voice sounded in his ear over the comms system. "Coming up on the Elysium."

Julia slowed to a stop, hovering in the water in front of him. Nick and Braden appeared next to her and pointed to the surface where the Elysium sat low and heavy in the water.

They were near the vessel's bow, its lights cast into the water like glittering gems.

"Everybody good?" He looked at Julia when he asked the question, searching her eyes through the mask for any sign of difficulty.

"I'm good." Julia's voice was clear and calm.

He held her gaze before looking at Braden.

"All good."

"Nick?" They hadn't talked much after their conversation on the terrace, and now he wished that he'd taken more time to tell Nick how much their relationship, their shared history, meant to him.

"A-okay," Nick said.

"Wait until I give you the all clear," Ronan said. "Keep an eye on the current."

It was easy to let an underwater current carry you off course. They would need to watch the Elysium to make sure they stayed in position.

He took a last look at Julia and killed his light before he ascended. There was no way to know the position of the guards while he was underwater, and he was careful to surface quietly, staying in the shadow of the bow until he could get his bearings.

The bow of the Elysium rose twenty feet overhead, hardly moving in the water. He didn't see anyone on deck, and he allowed himself a minute to take in the rest of the vessel, long, sleek, and ultra-modern.

The bridge rose into the night sky, the boat's antenna shining red, announcing its presence to other boats and low-flying aircraft.

A few seconds later, footsteps sounded on the bow.

"Save me some of that ouzo," a gruff voice said. After a pause, the man laughed and spoke again, this time from the other side of the bow. "Fuck you."

The footsteps receded and Ronan marked the time on his dive watch. While he waited, he untied the rope looped around his waist and grasped onto the hook on one end.

He swam a few feet away from the boat and tried to gauge the force and trajectory necessary to hit one of the bow's metal railings. He was on his fifth attempt — casting out the rope, listening to the clink and miss, pulling it back through the water to try again — when the hook finally caught on the railing.

He held onto the rope and sank under the surface, his eyes searching for the lights that marked Julia, Nick, and Braden's position. He found them right away only a few feet from where he'd left them.

He flashed his own light to make sure they could see him. "We're clear and tied on," he said into the comms system. "One guard so far, and I don't know when he'll be back, so be quick and keep it quiet."

Their lights rose toward him like fireflies. He waited until they'd reached his position and surfaced with them.

They pulled off their masks.

"Everybody good?"

They nodded.

"Let's wait."

They treaded water in silence. When footsteps sounded on the bow again, Ronan checked his watch: twenty minutes since the last check.

He held up two fingers, then a fist to indicate that the guards were working in twenty-minute intervals on deck.

The guard wasn't talking to anyone this time, and Ronan held his breath as the footsteps paused at the edge of the bow. The scent of cigarette smoke drifted downward.

The motherfucker was stopping for a smoke break.

Ronan looked at Julia, watching her for signs of fatigue, but she seemed okay.

A cigarette butt landed in the water a few feet from Ronan's position and the guard's footsteps moved around to the other side of the bow, disappearing toward the back of the boat.

Ronan held out the line for Braden, who would climb first to keep the deck clear while everyone else ascended.

He stripped off his mask and oxygen tank, then kicked off his flippers. He reached for the rope as the gear sank through the water and started climbing, using his bare feet as leverage on the side of the boat.

He was aboard the boat less than two minutes later.

Nick followed suit and Ronan handed the rope to Julia.

"Just drop everything?" she asked.

He heard the fear in her voice, and he understood it. Once they dropped the scuba gear, there was no way off the Elysium without one of the small motorboats attached the yacht.

But they'd been over it a hundred times, and there was no other way. It would be too difficult to climb with the gear. More importantly, they had no place to stash it on board the Elysium, and leaving it in plain sight wasn't an option for obvious reasons.

"Just drop it," he said. "It'll be okay. You've got the rope and you'll be on the boat in no time."

She hesitated, water beading on her face, and he wanted nothing more than to take her in his arms, kiss the salt from her lips, and tell her that she was safe.

Except he couldn't tell her that, because it would be a lie. It had been a lie since the moment they'd entered the water.

She dropped her face masl. Her oxygen tank went next, followed by the flippers.

"Remember," Ronan said, "climb as fast as you can before your arms get fatigued."

They'd practiced, but only on the smaller boat they'd been using for their dives. The Elysium's bow was four times as high off the water.

She grabbed onto the rope and hung for a few seconds before her feet made contact with the bow. Then she started moving, surprisingly fast, pulling herself hand over hand up the rope.

She was only a few feet from the top of the bow when she seemed to tire.

Nick's head appeared over the side. He reached out a hand. "Come on, Julia. Your sister's waiting."

She resumed the climb, hanging when she was within reach of Nick's hand, then reaching out for it.

"I've got you," he said, hauling her on board.

Ronan dumped his dive equipment and grabbed

the rope. When he climbed aboard the Elysium, the others had already put on the thin, rubber-soled dive shoes Braden had packed in the waterproof pouch at his side.

He handed a pair to Ronan.

He slipped them on. They would be safer than bare feet and provide better grip, but they'd also allow them to move quietly on the ship.

Braden reached into the bag he'd carried through the water and removed their weapons. He quickly handed them each a gun, keeping the additional equipment for him and Nick, who would be dealing with the guards while Julia and Ronan looked for Elise.

"Everybody set?" Ronan asked.

They nodded.

"See you on the flip side," Braden said, moving starboard.

Nick started along the port side of the boat, weapon drawn. Ronan moved with Julia into position behind him.

32

Julia stepped behind Ronan into an unlit room at one side of the boat. When her eyes adjusted to the dim light, she saw that the shadows lurking at the edges of the room were exercise equipment — treadmills, ellipticals, stationary bikes — plus a few weight machines.

They'd left Nick on the stern after he'd dispatched one of the guards with a quick hit of his gun to the man's head followed by a bullet, muffled by the weapon's silencer.

Nick had thrown him over the side of the boat with a surprising lack of fanfare and waved Ronan and Julia belowdeck.

They'd moved through an empty but luxurious lounge area before ducking into the exercise room.

So far the boat was oddly silent — no music, no crowds, and no guards, none but the one Nick had killed at the rear of the boat and whoever Braden had encountered on the other side.

Ronan waved her forward toward a door at one end of the exercise room. She called up the images of the boat's interior and thought the door led to a hall that would take them farther belowdeck to the sleeping cabins.

Ronan kept his weapon in position and pulled open the door. She expected to move in behind him, then heard the muffled thump of his silencer. When she looked around his broad shoulders, a large man in black was slumped on the floor of the hall, a smear of blood almost blending into the wallpaper behind him.

"Cover me," Ronan said, bending to grasp the dead man under the armpits.

Julia stepped in front of him and raised her weapon while Ronan dragged the man into a bathroom as big as Julia's apartment in Boston.

He stepped back into the hall and shut the door. "Let's keep moving."

They moved slowly down the hall, Ronan in the lead, weapon drawn. They passed a sauna, a media room, and what looked like a small spa, complete with two massage tables.

Julia was bothered by the silence. It felt wrong somehow, like they were on an empty boat drifting through an alternate universe where no one existed in the world but them.

Murmured voices rose at the end of the hall, and Ronan waved her back against the wall, both of them listening.

The voices were coming from a room up ahead, one they would have to pass to get to the sleeping cabins, and Ronan held up a hand, indicating that she should stay put while he checked it out.

She watched as Ronan approached the room at the end of the hall, her weapon slick in her hand, sweat coating the grip.

He stopped at the edge of the doorway, then leaned in to get a look. She held her breath and a moment later he waved her forward.

She moved quietly down the hall, grateful for the dive shoes. She couldn't resist a glance as she slipped past the partially open door, but once she'd looked, she wished she hadn't.

The room was some kind of computer center, large displays ticking down the time while in one corner dollar values rose next to asset numbers. Three men manned the screens, their backs turned to the door while they tapped at keyboards and touch screens and murmured into their headsets.

One of the men seemed to be videoconferencing with a suited man onscreen, although Julia couldn't hear their conversation.

"Don't think about it," Ronan said grimly as they descended a short staircase to the sleeping cabins belowdeck.

They entered another long hall, this one with closed doors on either side. According to the blueprints, this was where the bedrooms were, the most likely place for Elise to be kept prisoner.

Ronan tried one of the doors but Julia could see that it was locked.

She removed the pick set from a zipper in her wet suit and held it up with a question in her eyes.

Ronan shook his head and mouthed the words, "Not yet."

He moved down one side of the hall, trying the doors. Julia moved to the other side, doing the same thing. She was on the last door when a familiar voice spoke behind her.

She froze, then turned to face the door Ronan

was trying to open, the voice an urgent whisper behind it.

"Hello? Is anyone there? My name is Elise Berenger. I'm an American and I'm being kept here against my will. Please help me."

33

Ronan had barely registered the voice of the woman behind the door when something exploded from the back of the boat. The explosion was followed by a series of shouts and the thud of footsteps making their way toward the explosion.

"Elise! It's me." Julia was flattened against the door as if she might be able to materialize through it through sheer force of will. "It's Julia. I'm going to get you out of here."

Gunfire erupted from the front and back of the boat.

"Uh... I hate to ask, but we could use some help out here." Nick's voice was staticky in Ronan's ear.

He looked down the hall and back at Julia.

"Go!" she said. "I'll get Elise and meet you at the motorboat."

"No fucking way." He took a step back, preparing to kick in the door. "Stand back, Elise."

"Wait!" Julia put a hand on his wrist. "If we make noise, they'll come." She held up the pick set. "Go help Nick and Braden. I'll meet you."

He shook his head. "No."

Another round of gunfire blew through the boat and the lights flickered in the hall.

She looked in his eyes. "Do you trust me?"

He wanted to say no. He wanted to say he didn't trust anyone but himself to get her off the Elysium alive.

But that would be the end of them. And besides, it wasn't true.

He did trust her. Whether or not he trusted her wasn't the right question. The question was, did he love her enough to let her go?

"I trust you," he said.

"Then go. I'm right behind you." She held up her gun. "And I know how to use this."

He hesitated and shook his head. "Fuck me." He kissed her hard and fast. "You better be there, Julia. I'm not leaving without you."

She shoved him and he headed back up the flight of stairs as another explosion rocked the boat.

"Oh my god..." Elise was sobbing on the other side of the door. "Julia? Is that really you?"

"It's me," Julia said, choosing a pick from the pick set. "But I need you to be quiet while I open this door."

The pick was too big. She cursed and chose another one. Still too big.

Footsteps pounded above her and a moment later a tall man with dark curly hair appeared at the top of the stairs leading to the hall where she stood.

She raised her weapon and fired without thinking, hitting him square in the chest. She could only assume from the blood that blossomed on his shirt as he stumbled back into the hall that he wasn't wearing a vest.

"I thought I was dead, Julia. I thought I would never see you again. I thought — "

"Seriously, Elise, I need you to be quiet."

She fitted another pick into the lock. This one felt just right, and she turned it slowly, forcing herself not to rush, feeling for the tumblers as they cleared the pick.

Time seemed to slow, like she was moving

through a sea of molasses, gunfire coming from all corners of the boat, the crash of breaking glass making its way through the halls.

The lock gave way with a soft click. Julia turned the knob. Then she was pulling her sister into her arms, both of them crying and talking at the same time.

She pulled back to get a better look, hardly daring to believe the woman in front of her was her sister. But yes, it was Elise, thinner and with bruises on her neck and arms, her blond hair stringy and two inches longer.

But alive.

Elise's eyes dropped to Julia's gun.

Julia took her hand. "Do exactly what I say." Elise's eyes were blank, and Julia wondered if she was in shock. "Do you hear me, Elise? You do everything I say."

Elise nodded.

"Stay behind me."

Julia moved in front of her sister and stepped into the hall.

∽

Ronan had lost track of how many times he'd used his gun, how many guards had taken one of his bullets to the head or chest. He'd seen Nick take a hit to the calf, but his brother kept moving, so Ronan could only assume it was a minor wound.

Braden was somewhere on the bridge, the only sign of his presence the occasional firing of his silenced gun, barely audible in the chaos of the fighting at the rear of the boat.

He had no sense of how much time had passed since he'd left Julia in the hall outside the sleeping cabins. He was biding his time, lending a hand to Nick and Braden until the moment when he would be forced to go back in after Julia and Elise.

He caught sight of Nick using one of his vicious upper cuts on a short, stout guard. Nick kicked the man backward, waiting for him to hit the railing before he fired his weapon into the man's head.

The guard tipped over the side of the boat, disappearing into the darkness.

Ronan turned to find another guard advancing, this one wielding a wicked knife.

Ronan hated knives — which was why he always brought a gun.

He pointed his weapon at the man's head and fired.

Julia had just passed the computer room when Elise emitted a strangling sound behind her. She turned to find her sister's head locked in the arms of a massive man with a shaved head, an earring glinting in one ear, his eyes bulging and wild.

Julia shoved her gun against the man's throat. "Let her go."

He loosened his grip and stepped back, and Julia fired into his head.

Elise's scream went on and on.

Julia held her sister's face in her hands. "If you want to live, you'll shut up and keep moving."

The gunfire was louder now that they were closer to the back of the boat, and Julia could hear crashing overhead that could only mean someone was fighting on the bridge.

She kept her weapon ready and tried not to think about how easy it had been to kill someone, how eager she was to do it again. All the pain and frustration of the past months was leaking out of her, unleashed on the men trying to keep her from leaving with her sister.

She kept her weapon raised and moved,

expecting another obstacle around every corner, ready to deal with it when it came.

~

Ronan tipped the dead man into the water and turned to see Braden racing down the stairs from the bridge, blood leaking from a cut above his left eye.

"One of the crew got off a radio message before I got rid of him," he said. "I'm guessing reinforcements are on the way."

The sudden quiet was deafening. Either they'd dealt with all the guards on the boat or there were others belowdeck, mobilizing for another attack.

"How long?" Nick asked.

"Hard to say." Braden stepped onto the deck. "But we should get out of here."

"Get the boat ready," Ronan said, heading for the Elysium's interior. "Don't leave without us."

He was almost to the first set of stairs when Julia emerged from belowdeck. She stepped into the lounge off the stern, dragging a hollow-eyed Elise behind her. "What are we waiting for? Let's get the hell out of here."

Ronan looked at Braden and Nick. "You heard her. Let's go."

"I'll get rid of the second boat," Braden said, heading for the boat's port side.

Ronan made his way to the motorboat suspended on the starboard side. He used the button to lower the boat until it was level with the deck of the Elysium.

He helped Elise and Julia into the boat, then waited while Nick climbed in after them. A splash sounded from the other side of the ship and Braden reappeared alongside Ronan.

"Get in," Ronan said.

"Someone has to stay and lower the boat," Braden said.

Ronan held his gaze. "I'm aware."

"Get in the boat, Ronan." It was Julia's voice, and he forced himself not to look at her.

"We don't have time to argue," Ronan said. "I'll do exactly what you would do — lower the boat and jump in after you. You can pull me aboard."

Braden had barely stepped into the boat when Ronan pushed the button. The last thing he saw was Julia glaring at him, tears leaking down her cheeks.

He watched over the side until the boat hit the water. Nick started the motor and maneuvered it away from the Elysium.

Ronan stepped over the railing, wondering how

long it had been since the Elysium's crew had radioed for help, wondering if they'd have time to get away before helicopters shone spotlights over the water around the Elysium.

There was nothing to do but jump.

34

Ronan sat on a rock by the river and watched as Julia and Elise picked their way upstream, Chief sniffing the ground around them. Julia stood close to her sister, assuming a protective posture Ronan had become familiar with in the month since they'd returned from Greece.

They were in the woods surrounding John Taylor's house outside the city. The place seemed to be a comfort to Elise, and Julia had taken to walking with her sister in the evenings as the summer wore on, the days getting longer and hotter.

Sometimes Ronan stayed at the house, pretending to listen to John's stories about the Army when he was really counting the minutes Julia and Elise had been gone, forcing himself not to trail them through the woods just to make sure they were safe.

It was an impulse that had gotten even more powerful in the week since Julia received an unmarked envelope on the doorstep of the apartment she shared with Elise.

Ronan hadn't wanted them to return to the apartment at all. He'd argued that there was plenty of room at the Murphy house, that Julia and Elise would be safer there.

But Julia had thought it best for Elise to be in familiar surroundings, alone with her sister while she processed everything that had happened to her. In the end, Ronan had forced himself to let Julia go, to have faith in their love the way he'd asked her to have faith in it the night before they'd rescued Elise.

He'd buried himself in work during the time they'd been apart, knowing Julia needed the time with her sister, and just as important, that Elise needed the time to recover. Then Julia had received the photographs of her mother and grandfather, along with the one that had stopped Ronan's heart, a picture of Julia on the street outside her apartment just two days before.

Her voice had shook when she called to tell him, and he'd brought her and Elise to the house he shared with his brothers that same night. They'd been there ever since, rarely leaving except to go to the beach with Ronan and Chief and to visit their grandfather. Nick and Declan didn't seem mind, and Ronan had come to enjoy the fact that the house was full.

In spite of the circumstances, it felt like home.

He watched as Julia and Elise paused at the bank of the river. Julia reached into the shallow water and pulled out a rock that she handed to her sister. Elise took it and put it in her pocket without looking at it.

She'd become more morose as time wore on, as if the weight of her experience was finally hitting her. At first, she'd been in shock, alternating between manic euphoria and wordless tears, but she'd grown quieter and more disconnected with each day that passed. The shadows under her eyes hadn't subsided, and she was still painfully thin.

They'd filed a police report. They'd even talked to the FBI on the record, downplaying MIS's rescue mission to avoid too many questions.

But Ronan wasn't hopeful. Elise had been taken off the street not by Seth Campbell, but by someone she hadn't recognized, though no one doubted that Campbell groomed Elise as a target.

The FBI would look into the Elysium and its

ownership, but Manifest hadn't escaped detection so long for nothing: they were well-versed in remaining above the law.

John Taylor had pulled Ronan aside the first time Ronan accompanied Julia and Elise to the little cottage in the woods. The older man had made it clear that in his mind, MIS's mission wasn't complete. The job had never been just to rescue Elise — it had been to make the people who took her pay.

Ronan needed no encouragement. The locked doors on board the Elysium remained fresh in his mind, and he couldn't help wondering if there had been more women behind them, if the women had been drugged to keep them quiet.

If that hadn't been enough, the photographs left on Julia's doorstep sealed the fate of the men behind Manifest. They were a clear threat to Julia, and that was something that would never stand.

Julia shrieked and he looked up, his heart racing, to find that Chief had waded into the river, shaking off her wet fur onto Julia and Elise.

She looked at him and waved, then started back toward him with Elise.

Chief trotted ahead of them and put her paws on Ronan's thigh before giving his cheek a sloppy lick.

"Good girl, Chief." He ruffled her fur and stood as Julia and Elise came closer.

Julia slid her hand into his. "Hey, you."

He bent to kiss her. "Hey, yourself." He looked at Elise. "Ready to head back?"

They were still getting used to each other, but he hoped she felt safe with him, hoped she knew Ronan and his brothers would never let anyone hurt her again.

"Ready."

He held tight to Julia's hand as they headed back to the house. He hadn't known it was possible for someone to so totally occupy his heart and soul. At times their love still felt tenuous, but it always took his breath away.

Would he ever stop worrying about her? Waiting for another threat? Another shoe to drop?

Not until the men behind Manifested paid. And pay they would. He was going to burn their organization to the ground.

Then he was going to spend the rest of his life giving Julia everything.

His body. His heart. His soul.

Everything.

Thank you for reading Murphy's Wrath. Ronan and Julia's story concludes with Murphy's Love. Find out what happens when the identify of Manifest's leader is finally revealed and Julia makes a stunning discovery that will change her relationship with Ronan forever.

Murphy's Love is available now

Did you enjoy this book? Please help other readers find it by leaving a review.

Visit www.michellestjames.com and join the Michelle St. James reader group for book news and freebies.

Please find me online. I'd love to get to know you!

Website
Facebook
Twitter
Instagram
Bookbub
Syndicate Sinners Facebook Reader Group

ALSO BY MICHELLE ST. JAMES

Ruthless

Fearless

Lawless

Muscle

Savage

Primal

Eternal

Covenant

Revenant

Rule

The Sentinel

Rogue Love

Rebel Love

Fire with Fire

Into the Fire

Through the Fire

Eternal Love

King of Sin

Wages of Sin

The Awakening of Nina Fontaine

The Surrender of Nina Fontaine

The Liberation of Nina Fontaine

Thicker Than Water

Blood in the Water

Hell or High Water

Murphy's Wrath

Murphy's Love

Made in United States
Orlando, FL
01 April 2022